Elizabeth Bisla

The Secret Life Be
Heret

o u t l o o k

Elizabeth Bisland

The Secret Life Being the Book of A Heretic

1st Edition | ISBN: 978-3-75234-137-9

Place of Publication: Frankfurt am Main, Germany

Year of Publication: 2020

Outlook Verlag GmbH, Germany.

Reproduction of the original.

THE
SECRET LIFE

Being

THE BOOK OF
A HERETIC

JUNE 21.
L'Enfant Terrible.

"The very Devil's in the moon for mischief:
There's not a day, the longest, not the twenty-first of June,
Sees half the mischief in a quiet way
On which three single hours of moonlight smile."

At my age, alas! one no longer gets into mischief, either by moonlight or at midsummer, and yet to-day all the tricksey spirits of the invisible world are supposed to be abroad—tangling the horses' manes, souring the milkmaid's cream, setting lovers by the ears. Some such frisky Puck stirs even peaceable middle-aged blood at this season to mild little secret sins, such as beginning a diary in which to set down one's private naughty views—the heresies one has grown too staid and cautious to give speech to any longer.

All, I think, have some Secret Garden where they unbind the girdle of conventions and breathe to a sympathetic listener the opinions they would repudiate indignantly upon the housetops; but I know of no such kindred soul —indeed my private views are so heretical that I should tremble to whisper them even into the dull cold ear of night, lest I should cause it to turn pink, and thereafter hymns would not purge it. Hence no resource remains to ease my bosom of its perilous stuff but the unprotesting innocence of the blank pages of a diary.

There is a story concerning the king of some ungeographical country, to whom came two adventurers of cynical tendencies, professing to be able— given a certain allowance of jewels and precious metals—to weave a garment of exceeding richness and of such subtle texture that no monarch on earth might hope to match it. Setting up a loom and providing themselves with ample materials from the Royal treasury, they went through the motions of stringing a warp and thereupon industriously threw empty shuttles back and forth.

When the king, accompanied by his court, was summoned to observe the progress of the famous web, the puzzled ruler could see nothing but an empty loom, but before the eager explanations of the enthusiastic weavers, who pointed out here a glowing dye, there a splendid pattern, and having regard to the non-committal countenances of the courtiers, the king nodded sagely and waited developments.

"Best of all, Sire," cried the cheerful rogues, "so magical is this robe we

2

weave, that only those can see it whose tongue has never uttered a lie, whose hands have never taken a bribe."

Rises thereupon instant chorus of praise of the beautiful fabric from a unanimous court. Next day a solemn procession through the streets of the capital to display to the world the magic robe. Amazed multitude staring at the king in pompous dishabille, but hearing the courtiers' admiring cries, no man willing to admit his own blindness—when up speaks Tiresome Child: "Mother, why does the king ride abroad in his shirt?"

General outburst of mortified veracity, and futile search for the discreetly vanished adventurers.

So ends the story. But nothing of the sort really took place. Instead, l'enfant terrible was slapped and put to bed, to meditate upon his ill-timed outspokenness, and next day, and all the days thereafter, sees what his companions see. I know, because I myself am that Tiresome Child, and because my uncomfortable eyes refuse to see the imaginary robe in which so many kings of this world are dressed I have spent a large part of my life in disgrace. At last and tearfully I have learned to hold my tongue, but when the tricksome spirits of Mid-summer Eve are abroad, I get out pen and paper and, where no pious ear can be violated, secretly vent my elderly naughtinesses. My respectable acquaintances will be all the safer in consequence that I have an inviolable confidant of the real thoughts that lie behind my but slightly wrinkled brow and unrevealing eyes. Thackeray once said, "If women's eyes could only be *dragged*, what queer things one might learn."… Ah, the Secret Life!—who among us can guess at the thoughts that are concealed behind the clear brows and frank-seeming eyes of even those nearest us?

We live our lives draped and masked in our own bodies; forcing those bodies to speak the words, perform the actions expected from them, while we dwell alone within, thinking and wishing what we never, or rarely, express. It is this that drives us to diaries—the need to somewhere, somehow, speak the truth in a world of conformable lies. It is of no use to slip aside our masks or raise our draperies for an instant, in the hope that our fellows will recognize a hand or an eye like their own, and that thereupon even one of our companions will invite us to come out from under our robe and walk about with him friendlily, without disguise. Instead our companion makes signs of distress and resentment through the veil of his concealment, and we hastily readjust the mask and domino and resist further temptation to find a heart akin.

"It takes," says Thoreau, "two to tell the truth—one to speak and another to hear."

Called upon once to help a grief-stricken mother to lay away the belongings

3

of a boy summoned suddenly out of life, we unearthed among his abandoned treasures a curious collection of odds and ends concerning which we could imagine no value that should have moved him to keep them by him. A shell, a bit of ribbon, a rusty nail; scraps of paper with a scribbled line or two; cuttings, whose printed words referred to nothing which seemed to bear in any way upon what we might guess of as touching his life.

"I thought I knew every fibre of his heart," cried the mother in sudden tears, "and yet of all these strange things he seems to have treasured so carefully I cannot divine the meaning of a single one!" A whole world of ambitions, interests, and sentiments foreign to her he had carried away into eternal silence.

If I shall have persistence sufficient to continue this Heretic Diary, I am afraid it will find itself stuffed with an equally absurd number of my secret loves and hates, of the intolerable opinions for which I have been slapped and put to bed, of all the sentimental rubbish I carry about with me in a fardel under my mask and domino—the poor inconsequential treasures of my secret life.

July 7.
An Optimistic Cynic.

Amiel's Journal:—I have been reading it with the half impatient interest which such books always arouse—in me at least. It is a more agreeable book, however, than Marie Bashkirtseff's disingenuous posings, or Rousseau's vulgar, insulting confidences. One is impatient with the bore who talks about himself when one is impatient to bore him about one's own self, and yet, somehow, one is fascinated by the hope of getting behind the mask of personality.

I learned to read French that I might possess the contents of the "Confessions." George Eliot called it the most interesting book she knew, which fired my ambition to read it. With the aid of a dictionary, the four great volumes were got through somehow, and when the task was accomplished, though I loathed Rousseau, I had enough French to serve roughly for both reading and speech.

What ambition and courage one had in those days! I studied French while I did the churning. Remembering the strength and persistency of that time I wonder that I have come to middle age and done nothing. Athletic trainers say that there is in every one only a fixed capacity for development. One may reach that limit readily, and once reached no toil or patience will ever carry the power of the muscles beyond it by the smallest part of a fraction. Mentally, the same probably holds good. My capacity was, no doubt, always small. So far as it went the cramping, unpropitious circumstances of youth had no power to chill it, but prosperity, leisure, opportunity, could not add one jot to its possibilities....

In all these journals what I find interesting is not so much what the writer says as what he reveals unintentionally.

The impression Amiel leaves upon the reader is that he was at least a gentleman—that he had a gentle soul; clean and modest, continent and grave. His melancholy seems neither so profound nor so touching as Mrs. Humphrey Ward and his other critics would have one believe. At least it is neither tragic nor torturing. He gives the impression of saying "I have no bread—but," he adds cheerfully, after a moment's reflection, "the Lord will provide."

He is not rebellious. In moments of the most real gravity, when he is face to face with death, he clings to the egotistic superstition that perhaps—most probably—there is somewhere some wise kind Power deeply interested in his

5

doings, his emotions, his future. He is profoundly convinced that it is important how he feels, how he bears himself. He has no sense at all of the blind nullity of things. He asserts this nullity to be unthinkable.

All this is surprising when one remembers the insistence of his commentators upon the intense modernity of his mind. Is this modern? I cannot see wherein it differs from the spirit of the past. Such natures were not uncommon in other centuries—as was the nature of Erasmus for example....

The man had no passion. He did not marry because, he says, he demanded perfection; could not find or give it, and therefore resigned himself cheerfully to celibacy. Passion, of course, would have blinded his eyes to imperfections; having none, his eyes were always clear.... It is perhaps in this passionlessness that he is most modern. Most of us no longer demand perfection. Knowing it to be unattainable, modern common sense cheerfully agrees to abandon desire for it. This is visible in our literature, in art, in love. No one reads or buys long poems any more, therefore the poets never contemplate a new Paradise Lost. No one paints heroic pictures, for they are not salable. The grandiose has no market and therefore grows obsolete. The law of supply and demand rules there as elsewhere. Passion and the perfection it longs and strives for is démodé.

July 20.
A Poet Sheep-rancher.

F—— is dead, and with the announcement by cable this morning comes a belated letter from M——, full of hope and encouragement. A sudden rally had made her believe in a possibility of recovery—no doubt it was that last flare which comes often just as the oil fails and the light is about to go out.

My mind has been full of amazement all day. It is so difficult to realize that a strong, aggressive personality is finally and definitely extinguished. I have been thinking of their odd, romantic story. He must have had great seductive power—not easily realizable now—to have come into her life and have persuaded her to abandon everything to follow him. I have heard her tell the story often. The tall young sheep-rancher from New Zealand, with his burning eyes and his pockets full of sonnets, appearing one morning, and she suddenly abandons her brilliant position, her jointure, her two orphan boys, and goes away, despite the furious outcries of her family and friends, with a man seven years her junior; goes into the wilderness with him, New Zealand of more than a quarter of a century ago being decidedly wilderness, yet she calls those the happiest years of her life—spent in a shanty fifty miles from the nearest neighbour! She likes to recall the wild scrambles among the mountains; the wrestles to save the sheep from the spring floods; the vigils; the dances to which they rode on mountain ponies, sixty or seventy miles; the makeshifts; the caring for flocks and shepherds in the stress of heat and cold, of sickness and sorrow; and the snow-bound nights beside the fire, when the sonnets came to the fore again. After all it was youth, and love, and adventure; why shouldn't she have been happy? And she was justified in her faith. When I came to know them the detrimental young sheep-rancher moved in a world of gilded aides-de-camp, with sentries and mounted escorts attending his steps, surrounded by tropical pomp and spacious luxury, and now, alas! he is but one more unit in the yearly tribute of flesh and blood demanded by England's Equatorial Empire.

A handsome, brilliant, charming creature. The generation is the poorer for the loss of his graceful, cynical wit. He belonged to the generation who formed their ideals of manners upon *Pelham* and *Vivian Grey*. It was Byronism translated into prose. M—— says he bore his sufferings—enormous sufferings—with the light and humorous courage with which it was the ideal of the fine gentleman of his period to face all unpleasant situations.

SEPTEMBER 4.
An Eaten Cake.

The S——s came in last night after dinner. They cling to the old fashion, common in England before the advent of afternoon tea, of having the tray brought in about ten o'clock, so I tried it to-night because of them, and found it not a bad idea.

Simple, agreeable folk they are, of what is called in Scotland the middle classes. That is to say, they follow some commercial calling: I am not sure of its exact nature. They are very well educated in just the way which differentiates the British middle-class education from the other sort—they speak several modern languages fluently, and know little of the classics. All their learning is sound, unornamental, utilitarian. Some reference was made to a kinsman in a foreign town which I had visited. I could not recall any association with the name until the elder brother said quite simply and without any self-consciousness:

"He is Jones of Jones & Co. (a large haberdasher in P——)—you may have been in his shop."

It was nicely done. I doubt if an American could have achieved it in quite the same way. If he had made the confidence it would have been made with bravado, or he would have explained that the shop was an "emporium."

The girl has such a good restful British calm about her—I felt it after she was gone. It arises, I think, from lack of any special interest in the impression she makes upon others. All the rest of us—we Americans—were desirous of being agreeable, amusing—of making a good effect. We were consciously sympathetic, consciously vivacious, consciously civil. She was just herself; we might take or leave her as she was. It never occurred to her to attempt to be different for our sakes. The result of it is very reposeful. One is always conscious of a sense of strain in American society for this reason. It is because of that desire to impress, to please, that American voices in conversation grow sharp and hurried, that American faces grow keen and lined. We have a tradition that English women are dull and bovine, but no doubt they make the better mothers because of it. They hoard their energies to give to their sons. They bring their children into the world with deep reserves of strength. I have often observed the great superiority of English men over Americans in the capacity for long, sustained, unflinching labour. I am sure they owe that to the immense fund of unexhausted power given them by their mothers, who are profound wells of calm vitality. It is the old story of being unable to eat one's cake and have it too. American women eat their cake in the form of a higher exhilaration in existence, but when the drain of creation comes they have nothing save nervous energy to give. The rest of the cake has already been devoured. There are no reserves for the child to call upon.

I believe that Englishmen—without reasoning upon the matter—feel this instinctively. They vastly prefer their own women as mates. I have rarely known an Englishman to marry an American woman who had not the extrinsic attraction of wealth. They do not hesitate to marry penniless countrywomen of their own.

September 12.
Concerning Elbows on the Table.

A—— was here to-day. What a formal little soul it is! She can never begin where she left off. One has her acquaintance to make all over again each time she comes.

The depths, the heights of her propriety!... Always that extremely well behaved look, which never changes. P—— says, "A—— is too modest to take off and put on expressions in public."

One wonders if there is any privacy so entire that she would consider dishevelment of behaviour permissible. How exhausting to herself such flawless respectability must become!

She is the concentrated essence of the bourgeoisie. A savage can be natural; he knows nothing else, but when his eyes are opened and he sees himself to be naked the reign of the fig-leaf begins. There is something pathetic in that long era of profound distrust of his own nature and impulses. What does he think he would do if he let himself go?

Perhaps he is, underneath all that propriety, still so close to savagery that he dare not trust himself to be natural lest he instantly relapse into barbarism. After many generations of breeding he dare be savage and free again if he like —he is so sure of himself. As Mrs. B—— says, he becomes at last "A man who can afford to put his elbows on the table."

When he reaches such a point I notice he is always impatient of the constraint of those still bound by the shackles of self-conscious propriety, forgetting that he owes his own freedom to many generations that laboured in bonds, struggling to slay or subdue the savage....

OCTOBER 14.
An Autumn Impulse.

A bird sat on the balcony rail just outside my window to-day gossiping with an unseen neighbour perched somewhere out of my range of vision. He was rather a grimy little person, and as the day was cold he made a perfect puff ball of himself. I listened to them conversing with great interest, feeling, as I always do when I hear birds talk, that if I only paid a little closer attention it would be possible to understand all they say. It is somewhat the same sensation one has in overhearing a rapid dialogue in French which one is too lazy to try to follow. When I came through I think I left some of the doors ajar behind me, and I remember my bird avatar especially clearly. Even yet, when autumn comes, I am pursued by a fluttering longing to arise and go southward. I feel that something beautiful—some wide splendid ecstasy is calling me if I will only go to meet it. I can remember having that sensation in my earliest childhood. In my dreams I often fly, with beautiful swoopings and balancings, with sudden confident droppings, through the elastic air, and sometimes I am in an enclosed place, beating my wings against the bounds, knowing no other way to get out....

When I look at birds they seem to know me. Not in the way of a mere creature who puts out crumbs in convenient breakfasting places, or who brings strawberries to one's cage, but they meet my eye with that familiarity one sees in the glance of brothers—a look of mutual understanding. My own sense is of kinship of the closest character. I understand how they regard things—what they think and feel. I wish I could so concentrate my attention as to catch what this grimy little citizen is saying to his fellow on the nearby ledge. If I could, what a flood of other memories it would restore that are now dim and confused.

NOVEMBER 1.
John-a'-Dreams.

I dreamed last night that I wore upon my breast a great necklace of flat golden plates cut in the shape of winged things, and these were linked together with other flat plates of turquoise. My garments were of white semi-transparent stuff, and my limbs and body showed through it. Before me stood a building of some sort, creamy yellow in colour and of a style of architecture with which I am not familiar—though it seemed familiar enough to me in my dreams. Now I have only a confused sense of low domes set upon massive cubes. I was waiting for the sun to rise. The air was warm and dry and that white glamour of the dawning light lay upon the surrounding country, which seemed flat and not very verdant. Suddenly the rays of the sun, which rose apparently immediately behind this dome, spread out about it like an aureole (Gavin Douglas's "Golden fanys")—and this seemed a signal for me to lift my arms above my head and recite a sort of litany—and then—it all passed away....

Most of one's dreams are confused and blurred by a sense of conflicting personalities. There is generally a sort of impression that while the incidents are apparently happening to one's self, they are happening in reality to some other being, not quite one's self; but this one was very clear, with no arrière pensée. I have worked out a theory which seems to me to quite solve the mystery of dreams.

Lifelong familiarity with the phenomena of sleep—with the trooping phantoms that inhabit slumber's dusk realm—has so dulled our wonder at the mystery of our double existence of the dark that night after night we open with calm incuriousness the door into that ghostly underworld, where we hold insane revels with fantastic spectres, babble with foolish laughter at witless jests, stain our souls with useless crime, or fly with freezing blood from the grasp of unnamable horrors, and with the morning we saunter serenely back from these adventures into the warm precincts of the cheerful day, unmoved, unstartled, and forgetting.

The hypnotists, because they can make a man feel pain or pleasure without material cause, are gaped upon with awed surprise by the same man who once every twenty-four hours of his life, with no more magic potion than healthy fatigue, with no greater weapon for wonder working than a pillow, may create for himself phantasmal illusions beside which all mesmeric suggestions are but the flattest of commonplace.

The naive egotism of superstition saw in the movements of the solar system only prognostications concerning its own bean crop, and could discern nothing in the dream-world but the efforts of the supernatural powers to communicate, in their usual shuffling and incompetent fashion, with man. The modern revolt from this childishness has swung the pendulum of interest in dreams so far up the other curve of the arc that there seems now to be a foolish fear of attaching any importance whatever to the strange experiences of sleep, and as a result an unscientific avoidance of the whole subject. The consequence of this absurd revulsion is that in a period of universal investigation one of the most curious functions of the brain is left unexamined and unexplained.

Some dabbling there has been, with results of little more value than were the contents of the greasy, bethumbed dream-books of the eighteenth-century milkmaid or apprentice. The labour bestowed upon the matter has been mainly directed to efforts to prove the extreme rapidity with which dreams pass through the mind, and that it is some trivial outward cause at the very instant of awakening—such as a noise, a light, or a blow—which rouses the brain to this miraculous celerity of imaginative creation.

The persistent assertion that a dream occurs only at the moment of awakening shows how little real attention has been given to the matter, since the most casual observation of "the dog that hunts in dreams" would have shown that he may be "chasing the wild deer and following the roe" in the grey Kingdom of Seeming without breaking his slumbers. He will start and twitch, and give tongue after the phantom quarry he dreams he is pursuing, and yet continue his sleep without an interval. But have it whichever way one likes, the heart of the mystery is not yet discovered. How do they explain why a noise or a gleam of light—such as the waking senses know familiarly—should at this magical moment of rousing cause the brain to create with inconceivable rapidity a crowd of phantasmagoria in order to explain to itself the familiar phenomena of light and sound?

Dr. Friederich Scholz, in his recent volume upon "Sleep and Dreams," gives an example of rapid effort of the mind to explain the sensations felt by the sleeping body:

"I dreamed of the Reign of Terror, saw scenes of blood and murder, appealed before the Revolutionary Tribunal, saw Robespierre, Marat, Fouquier-Tinville, all the personages of that time of horrors, argued with them, was finally, after a number of occurrences, condemned to death, was carried to the place of execution on a cart through enormous masses of people, was bound by the executioner to the board. The knife fell and I felt my head severed from my body. Thereupon I awoke and found that a loosened rod of the bed had fallen on my neck like the knife of the guillotine, and this had happened, my mother assured me, at the very moment when I awoke.".…

That the mind should, merely because of the body's sleep, be able to *create* a whole scene of a terrible drama with a rapidity impossible when all the functions are awake and active is incredible. The only function of the brain capable of this lightning-like swiftness of vision is *memory*. To create requires a certain effort, consumes a certain period of time, but a scene once beheld, an adventure once experienced and vividly impressed upon the memory, can be recalled in its minutest details in a period of time too short to be reckonable.

That the sensitive plate of the brain never loses any clear picture once received, has been demonstrated beyond doubt. The picture, the sensation, may be overlaid and hidden for a long time beneath the heaps of useless lumber that the days and years accumulate in the mind's storehouse, but need or accident, or a similarity of circumstance, will bring the forgotten belonging to light—sometimes with startling effect. There is the well-known instance of a girl who, during an attack of fever delirium, spoke in a language that no one about her could understand. Investigation proved it to be Welsh—a language of which, both before and after her illness, she was totally ignorant. Further investigation showed that being born in Wales she had understood the tongue as a very little child, but had afterwards completely forgotten it.

It is commonly known that in the struggle of the body against death by water, the memory, stirred to furious effort, produces all her stores at once— probably in the frantic endeavour to find some experience which may be of use in this crisis.

It is often broadly asserted that the memory retains each and every experience which life has presented for its contemplation, but this is hardly true. The memory makes to a certain extent a choice, and chooses oftentimes with apparent caprice. To demonstrate the truth of this, let one endeavour to recall the first impression retained by his childish mind and it usually proves to be something extremely trivial. My own first clear memory is a sense of the comfort to my tired little two-year-old body of the clean linen sheets of the bed at the end of a perilous and adventurous journey, of whose startling incidents my memory preserved only one. Often this capricious faculty will seize upon some few high lights in a vivid picture and reject all the unimportant details. As a rule, however, it is the profound stirring of the emotions which wakes the memory to activity. A woman never forgets her first lover. A man to the end of his life can recall his first triumph, or his most imminent danger, and a trifle will often, after the lapse of half a century, fill the eye with tears, make the cheek burn, or the heart beat with the power of the long-passed emotion, preserved living and fresh by the memory.

That the memory uses in sleep the material it has gathered during the day, and during the whole life, no dreamer will deny; but here again it is capricious; some parts of the day's—the life's—experiences are used, others rejected. Added to these natural and explicable possessions of the memory are a mass of curious, conflicting, tangled thoughts, which are foreign to our whole experience of existence, and which, when confused with our own memories, makes of our nights a wild jumble of useless and foolish pictures. If it be true that it is by some outward impression upon the senses that dreams are evoked, that it is the endeavours of the somnolent mind to explain to itself the meaning of a noise, a light, a blow, which creates that delusion we call dreams, then it is not upon the stores of our own memories alone that the brain draws for material, since the falling rod awoke in the mind of Dr. Scholz a picture of the French revolution, which he had never seen, and different in detail and vividness from any picture his reading had furnished.

Heredity is an overworked jade, too often driven in double harness with a hobby; but the link between generation and generation is so strong and so close that none may lightly tell all the strands of which it is woven, nor from whence were spun the threads that tie us to the past. It is very certain, despite the theories of Weismann, that the acquired characteristics of the parent may be transmitted to the child. The boy whose father walked the quarter-deck is, nine times out of ten, as certain to head for salt water as a seagull born in a hen's nest. The victim of ill-fortune and prisoner of despair who breaks the jail of life to escape fate's malice leaves a dark tendency in the blood of his offspring, which again and again proves the terrible power of an inherited weakness. Women who lose their mind or become clouded in thought at childbirth—though they come of a stock of *mens sana*—transmit the blight of insanity to their sons and daughters both; and not only consumptive tendencies and the appetite for drink are acquired in a lifetime and then handed on for generations, but preferences, talents, manners, personal likeness—all may be the wretched burden or happy gift handed down to the son by the father. Who can say without fear of contradiction that the memories of passions and emotions that stirred those dead hearts to their centre may not be a part of our inheritance? The setting, the connection, is gone, but the memory of the emotion remains. Such and such nerves have quivered violently for such or such a cause—the memory stores and transmits the impression, and a similar incident sets them tingling again, though two generations lie between.

Certainly animals possess very distinctly these inherited memories. A young horse never before beyond the paddock and stables will fall into a very passion of fear when a snake crosses his path, or when driven upon a ferry to cross deep, swift water. He is entirely unfamiliar with the nature of the danger, but at some period one of his kind has sweated and throbbed in hideous peril, and the memory remains after the lapse of a hundred years. He, no more than ourselves, can recall all the surrounding circumstances of that peril, but the threatening aspect of a similar danger brings memory forward with a rush to use her stored warning. When the migrating bird finds its way without difficulty, untaught and unaccompanied, to the South it has never seen, we call its guiding principle instinct—but what is the definition of the word instinct? No man can give it. It but removes the difficulty one step backward. Call this instinct an inherited memory and the matter becomes clear. Such memories, it is plain, are more definite with the animals than with us; but so are many of their faculties, hearing, smell, and sight.

Everyone has felt many times in his life a sense of familiarity with incidents that have had no place in his own experience, and has found it impossible to offer any explanation for the feeling. Coming suddenly around a turn of a hill upon a fair and unknown landscape, his heart may bound with a keen sense of recognition of its unfamiliar outlines. In the midst of a tingling scene of emotion, a sensation of the whole incident being a mere dull repetition will rob it of its joy or pain. A sentence begun by a friend is recognized as trite and old before it is half done, though it refers to matters new to the hearer. A sound, a perfume, a sensation, will awaken feelings having no connection with the occasion.

The first day I ever spent in a tropical country I was charmed with the excessive novelty of everything about me; but suddenly that evening, being carried home in a chair by the coolie bearers, a flood of recognition poured over me like the waves of the sea, and for a few minutes the illusion was so strong as to leave me breathless with astonishment. I had the sense of having often done this before. The warm night, the padding of the bare feet in the dust, the hot smell of leaves, were all an old, trite experience. For days I struggled with that tormenting sense, with which we are all familiar, of being unable to recall a something, a name, that is perfectly well known—is "on the tip of the tongue," as one says—but all in vain; and in time the recognition grew fainter and more elusive with each effort to grasp it, until it slipped forever away into darkness. If such experiences as these are not inherited memories, what are they?

With sleep, the will becomes dormant. Waking, it guards and governs; chooses what we shall do and be and think; stands sentinel over the mind and rejects all comers with which it is not familiar. Unless the thought comes from within the known borders of the body's own life, the will will have none of it. But overtaken by fatigue and sinking into slumber with the night, his domain is left fenceless and unpatrolled, for with the will goes his troop of watchmen, judgment, logic, deliberation, ethics; and memory, ungoverned and uncontrolled, holds a feast of misrule. The barrier between past and present melts away; all his ancestors are merged into the individual; the events of the day are inextricably tangled with those of two centuries since, and this motley play of time is called a dream.

A man going back but to his great grandparents has already fourteen direct progenitors, and is heir of such strange or striking episodes of their fourteen lives as were sufficiently deeply impressed upon their memories to be transmittable. This alone is enough, one would think, to provide all the nights with material for the queer kaleidoscopic jumbling of leavings, with which the nimble mind diverts itself, turning over the leaves of its old picture-book alone in the dark while its sluggish comrade snores; but there is no reason to believe that there is a limit to these inheritances.

The most vivid sensation my night memory holds is of finding myself standing alone, high up in a vast arena. It is open to the sky and the night is falling swiftly and warm. Everyone has gone but myself, but there is a tremulous sensation in my mind, as of very recent excitement, noise, and tumult. I am waiting for someone who is coming through the arched door on the left, and I rise to go. I feel the rough coolness of the stone beneath my hand as I help myself to rise, and upon my throat and bosom I have a sensation of the light wool of my garment. It has the vivid familiarity of a personal and perfectly natural experience—so strong that, waking, I retain as keen a sense of it as if it were a happening of yesterday. I remember many more dreams of this type—momentary flashes of sensation of the trivial things about me, such as all persons have felt in their waking lives, only that the things about me in my dreams are totally unfamiliar to my waking brain. In one of these I am emerging from the back door of a small white house— intensely white in the glare of a fierce sun. The house seems square and flat-topped, built of stone and with no windows visible here in the rear. It opens on a narrow street of similar residences. A man is with me, dressed in a long black robe and wearing a curious black head-dress. He is reproaching me and remonstrating violently concerning my indifference in regard to religious matters. I look away, annoyed and bored by his vehemence, and the whole picture vanishes. It was as clear, as natural and familiar, as my own waking life, while it lasted…. The narrow street of white houses seemed the only possible form for a street. I had no consciousness of anything different or more modern. The man's eager, stern face, with the heavy beard and the high head-dress, looked in no way strange or unfamiliar. With that double consciousness with which we are all familiar when awake, I watched the movement of his lips and the wagging of his beard as he talked, full of a sense of distaste, and thought, while listening to his flow of clear words, "How tiresome these religious men are!"

Another time I was aware of standing in the dark, sword in hand (I seemed to be a man and the seeming was not strange to me), listening with furious pulses to a confusion of clashing blades and stamping of feet. Under the surface of passionate excitement the deeper sub-consciousness said: "All is lost! The conspiracy is a failure!" I was aware of a cool bravado which recognized the uselessness of attempting escape. The dice had been thrown— they had turned up wrong, that was all. Yet so vigorous and courageous was the heart of this man that he was still buoyantly unafraid. There was a rush of bodies by him; the door swung back against him, crushing him to the wall, and a few moments later, under guard, he was passing through a long, low corridor of stone. The torches showed the groined arch above him, and, a cell being unlocked, for the first time he felt afraid. Inside was a big bear with a collar about its neck, and two villainous-faced mountebanks sat surlily upon the floor. The man was very much afraid at the thought of such companions, for his hands were tied and he had no sword; yet he reasoned jovially with his guards, not wishing to show his real terror. After some protests his sword was returned to him and he stepped inside, again cheerfully confident. The door clanged to behind him and the dream faded. All the conditions of the dream, the change of sex, the strange clothes and faces, the arched corridor, the men with the bear, seemed to my senses perfectly natural. They were quite commonplace, and of course. For the most part, however, my dreams are the fantastic hodge-podge common to dreamers, such as might result from the unsorted, unclassified memories of a thousand persons flung down in a heap together and grasped without choice. One curious fact I have noted is that though I am a wide and omnivorous reader, I have never had a dream or impression in sleep which might not have been part of the experience of some one of European or American ancestry. I am an ardent reader of travel and adventure, but never have I imagined myself in Africa, nor have the landscapes of my dreams been other than European or American.

Mr. Howells, in "True I Talk of Dreams," added confirmation on this point by saying that he had never been able to discover a dreamer who had seen in his dreams a dragon or any such beast of impossible proportions.

It suggests itself—*en passant*—that dragons and other such "fearful wild fowl" are not uncommon in the cataclysmic visions of delirium, but perhaps the potency of fever, of drugs, of alcohol, or of mania, may open up deeps of memory, of primordial memory, that are closed to the milder magic of sleep. The subtle poison in the grape may gnaw through the walls of Time and give the memory sight of those terrible days when we wallowed—nameless shapes —in the primæval slime. Who knows whether Alexander the Great, crowning himself with the gold of Bedlam's straws, may not be only forgetful of the years that gape between him and his kingly Macedonian ancestor? Even Horatio's philosophy did not plumb all the mysteries of life and of heredity.

Another interesting fact, in this connection, is that those who come of a class who have led narrow and uneventful lives for generations dream but little, and that dully and without much sensation; while the children of adventurous and travelled ancestors—men and women whose passions have been profoundly stirred—have their nights filled with the movement "of old forgotten far-off things and battles long ago." Again, it is a fact that many persons, while hovering on the borders of sleep, but still vaguely conscious, are accustomed to see pictures of all manner of disconnected things—many of them scenes or faces which have never had part in their waking life—drifting slowly across the darkness of the closed lid like the pictures of a magic lantern across a sheet stretched to receive them, and these, by undiscernible gradations, lead the sleeper away into the land of dreams, the dim treasure house of memory and the past.

If a dream is a memory, then the stories of their momentary duration are easily credible. The falling rod upon the sleeper's neck might recall, as by a lightning flash, some scene in the Red Terror in which his ancestor participated—an ancestor so nearly allied, perhaps, to the victim suffering under the knife as to know all the agonies vicariously, and leave the tragedy bitten into his memory and his blood forever.

When the words heredity or instinct are contemplated in their broad sense they mean no more than inherited memory. The experiences of many generations teach the animal its proper food and methods of defence. The fittest survive because they have inherited most clearly the memories of the best means of securing nourishment and escaping enemies. The marvellous facility gradually acquired by artisans who for generations practise a similar craft is but the direct transmission of the brain's treasures.

In sleep the brain is peculiarly active in certain directions, not being distracted by the multitude of impressions constantly conveyed to it by the five senses, and experiments with hypnotic sleepers prove that some of its functions become in sleep abnormally acute and vigorous. Why not the function of memory? The possessions which during the waking hours were useless, and therefore rejected by the will, surge up again, vivid and potent, and troop before the perception unsummoned, motley and fantastic; serving no purpose more apparent than do the idle, disconnected recollections of one's waking moments of dreaminess—and yet it may hap, withal, that the tireless brain, forever turning over and over its heirlooms in the night, is seeking here an inspiration, or there a memory, to be used in that fierce and complex struggle called Life.

NOVEMBER 6.
The Fountain of Salmacis.

G—— was talking yesterday about the "Sonnets from the Portuguese." Liked them. Thought them the high-water mark of Feminine Poetry....

Alas, then, for that capitalized variety of verse!

To me these sonnets are extremely disagreeable. There is a type of man whose love is intolerably odious in all its manifestations to a wholesome woman. She feels that he is too nearly akin to her own sex for his love to seem a natural, virile thing. Other men never appear to guess this cause of persistent lack of success with women.

They say: "Jones is a good fellow—modest, clean-minded, gentle,—why is he so unlucky with women? The truth is, women like brutes."

The underlying femininity of Jones is not repulsive to them. They probably feel, however, the same repugnance for the tendernesses of women who are too nearly akin to themselves.

The Greeks seem to have thought about and observed this. From their keen vision none of the phenomena of life, apparently, was hid, and they were quite aware of this occasional confusion of the nature and person of the sex. As usual they typified it and invented legends about it, though they were not, of course, aware of its cause—the atavistic tendency to throw back to the primordial condition when both sexes existed in the same individual; but then they were poets and not scientists. They got at essential truths by instinct and revealed their knowledge by beautiful suggestion rather than by exact analysis. The dry-as-dusts fail even yet to see that their marbles and legends are as valuable in the study of life as German theses.

"The Sonnets from the Portuguese" give me the unwholesome, uncomfortable sense that one gets from those unlucky feminine men and masculine women. They mingle in a disagreeable fashion the pride and reserve of the woman who receives worship and the abandon and aggressiveness of the man who sues.

One wonders why women cannot write poetry?—or rather, to speak with more exactness—are never poets. Once or twice in their lives, perhaps, they may speak with sacred fire, but they are never, in the full meaning of the word, poets. They cannot rise out of themselves.

Gosse says of Mrs. Browning: "She was not striving to produce an effect; she was trying with all the effort of which her spirit was capable to say exactly what was in her heart."

There is the whole secret of the feminine failure in art. It always degenerates into an attempt to express, not humanity, but the individual woman. Woman is inevitably personal. She still sits alone at the door of her wigwam. Of humanity, she is ignorant, and to it is, moreover, indifferent.

Mrs. Browning was only once shaken out of herself—when she wrote that fine plaint "De Profundis"—voicing the griefs of the many in telling of her own. After all, a portrait of one's self only is not art, or is art in its most limited form. Aurora Leigh and all the rest are simply Elizabeth Barrett masking under other names. However much the hand may resemble Esau's, the voice is always the voice of Jacob.

Byron had these same feminine limitations—"dressing up" (as the children say) as a Pirate, a Turk, or the like, and reciting a rhymed Baedeker for the benefit of the untravelled; but whether Pirate or Giaour, always unmistakably Byron.

What the women with poetic gifts *can* do is to translate delightfully. Mrs. Browning's translations of Heine are quite the best in existence. Emma Lazarus made an English version of "*Une Nuit de Mai*" that is almost more delightful than the original. She might have enriched our treasury of verse with priceless transferences; instead of which she wasted her gifts upon unimportant "expressions of herself."

NOVEMBER 20.
Two Siegfrieds.

A——— says there is no definite, abstract standard of beauty or perfection.

We were talking of Jean de Reszke's *Siegfried*. A——— was completely satisfied with it. I explained that he was so only because he had not seen Alvary in the part. A——— was sure that even if he had done so de Reszke might still be best to his taste; asserting again that there was no ideal good in art, but only preference. Of course he does say this for the very reason that I advanced—because he had not seen Alvary.

Poor beautiful young creature! He died recently in Germany in horrible, useless, ridiculous pain. Wagner, I am sure, would have thought him the ideal *Siegfried*, for he never made vocal gymnastics a fetish, but demanded satisfaction for the eye as much as for the ear.

Alvary's *Siegfried* was the very embodiment of splendid, golden, joyous youth. Balmung beaten into shape, he sprang from the forge, whirling it and laughing at its glitter as an ecstatic child might. The splitting of the anvil was the mere sudden caprice of youthful bravado and mischief. He looked about for an instant to find something on which to test his new toy, and struck the iron in half as a boy would snip off the head of a daisy with his new whip. All his movements had the unpremeditatedness of youth.

Drunk with the struggle and the triumph of his contest with the dragon, he killed *Mime* more to sate this new lust of power than to mete out justice or due punishment. He threw himself, sweating with exertion, and swelling with a new realization of his manhood, upon the grasses by the stream, and as the breezes cooled his body and spirit, and the soft peace of the green world stole upon him, romance woke in his face and voice: the rough uncouthness of boyhood fell away like a discarded garment.

Who that once saw and heard it can ever forget those fresh tones or that slim-waisted boy wandering away into the sunlit forest, his beautiful dreaming face lifted yearningly to the thrilling bird voice that sang of love?… Youthseeking passion—the sleeping woman ringed with fire.

Ah me!—all our hearts ached after him; after our own splendid moment.

It is useless to say that this is not absolute beauty. It is impossible that a heavy-footed tenor (whose belt would have served for a saddle girth) with a square Sclav head and pendulous cheeks can be equalized to the other by individual taste. Such taste is simply bad.

JANUARY 6.
A Door Ajar.

I have been reading Pater's "Greek Studies"; a volume which an amiable friend presented to me as a Christmas gift.

It affects me physically as well as mentally. I must lay the book down now and then, because I find my heart beats and my temples grow moist. It is as if its covers were doors opening into the other world—that world that is always just beyond one.

I don't know whether it is a common experience, but from my earliest childhood I have always had a sort of belief that if one stooped very low, held one's breath, and made a bold spring, one would break through and under the barrier, and be *There*!

Or one might go very suddenly around a corner and be *There*. Always there was the sensation that it was lying just beyond, just outside of one's self, and that only a certain heaviness of the flesh, a certain lack of concentration of attention, prevented one's participation in it.

Twice the door almost opened. I sprang in spirit to cross the threshold, and there was—nothing. The door was slammed in my face, but I never forgot that I had nearly got through. It was like death. As if one's brain and heart had suddenly grown vast and vapourized. Pater's book rouses some echo of those sensations.

I can't define what the other life is. It is all around me. I feel it in the water when I swim—a sentiency. If I could only look close enough into the shifting depths, I should see—a hand clasped quickly enough would grasp—what always just evades.

I feel it around me, breathing and watching in the woods. It is what I cannot quite catch in the talk of the birds. It is what the animals say with their eyes.

The Greeks understood it. They called it Pan, and Cybele, and Dionysus, or dryads in the woods, or nymphs in the fountain, but those were only terms by which they tried to express the inexpressible. It is so subtle—so intoxicating. It is like love—a reblending with all the elements of nature. One aches and strains toward it, and yet feels a delicious, shuddering reluctance to know.

JANUARY 7.
At Time of Death.

Oh High Heart of mine,
  Now list to a wonder!
Thou shalt vent thy great rages
  In lightning and thunder.
And the force of thy fury, more mighty than they,
Shall rock mountains, and rip them asunder.

When thou weepest, oh Heart!
  All thy bitter deploring
In the white whirling rains
  Shall have anguished outpouring.
And the salt and the sound of thy grief, like the sea,
Shake the night with its sullen wild roaring.

When thou lovest, oh Heart!
  Into sudden fierce flower,
'Neath thy passionate breath
  In one rapturous hour,
Earth shall blossom, all crimson and trembling with love,
Stirred to heart by thy rage and thy power.

Then, high Heart, be brave!
  This death is but rending
Of limits that vexed,
  And the ultimate blending
With the cosmical passions of Nature thine own,
Made immortal, insatiate, unending.

January 10.
The Curse of Babel.

Boutet de Monvel, who had been lending H—— a polite but obviously fatigued attention, got up with alacrity as the clock struck ten and bowed himself out, with that military bend of the hips characteristic of French salutes. H—— passed his handkerchief around the top of his collar and said:

"*Damn* Babel!"

We all laughed.

"Now, here," said H——, indignantly, "is a man with a beautiful mind, a man full of beautiful thoughts and visions, and because of those infernal French verb inflections, because they will call tables and chairs 'he' and 'she' instead of 'it,' I can't communicate with him without boring him to death. We English-speaking people are a great deal more lenient. Some of the pleasantest talks I've ever had have been with foreigners who waded through a slaughter of my native tongue to a positive throne in my respect. But no foreigner can ever tolerate broken French or Spanish. They jump to the immediate conclusion that a man who can't speak their abominable gibberish correctly must be either a boor or a fool, and they don't take the pains to conceal that impression. Why don't they learn to speak English, so that a human being could talk to them?"

R—— told a story of recent experience in Italy, which he thought suggested an equal arrogance in the Anglo-Saxon.

He had watched a young woman, an American, on the railway platform at Naples, explaining in lucid English to the porter her wishes concerning her luggage. The porter stared, shrugged, and seized a bag. The girl caught his arm.

"Put that down," she said sternly. "I mean that to go in the carriage with me. Those two trunks are to be labelled for Rome and put in the van."

The porter began to gesticulate and gabble.

"There's no use making so much noise," she commented contemptuously. "Just do as I tell you and don't lose time."

The Italian hunched his shoulders, threw his hands out in fan-like gestures, and made volcanic appeals to heaven. R——, who is shy, but chivalrous, and who speaks six Italian dialects, felt called upon to take part.

"Excuse me, Madam," he said, "but you seem to be having some difficulty with your luggage. As I speak Italian, perhaps I may be of service to you."

The girl turned a cold eye upon him and waved him away.

"Thank you," she said, "you are very kind, but all the world has got to speak English eventually, and there is no use indulging these people in their ridiculous Italian now!"

January 14.
The Fourth Dimension.

I lunched with Mary R—— yesterday and heard a curious story. Mrs. M——, who is ordinarily so amusing, seemed *distrait* and disturbed all through the meal, and when the other women had gone, Mary, who is extremely sensitive and sympathetic to the state of mind of everyone about her, led Mrs. M——, in a manner fascinating in its skilfulness, to unpack her overladen spirit.

She said: "I have been spending the morning with a friend, who is half mad with melancholia. She has had a terrible experience. She is a Philadelphia woman. Her husband was a manufacturer of window glass. He died about five years ago from typhoid fever and left her with a small fortune and two daughters; one fourteen years old, one seventeen—nice, rosy, wholesome, well brought up girls. They had always wanted to travel, but during her husband's lifetime he was too busy and she would never leave him. About a year after his death, they concluded, as the lease of their house had run out, to store their furniture and go abroad for a time, with the idea that the girls could perfect themselves in languages and music and see something of the world.

"I don't want you to think there was anything sensational about them. They were just quiet, middle-class Philadelphians,—you know the type,—modest, conventional, devoted to the proprieties. That's what makes their story all the more tragic.

"They arrived in London; took quiet lodgings in Dover Street, and concluded to spend six months in England, seeing the sights, and making these London lodgings their headquarters. They had been there all through the month of May, doing picture galleries, churches, and the museums, and occasionally a theatre. One Saturday they had tickets for a concert, and as the place was near and the day was fine, they decided to walk to the place where the concert was to be given, stopping at a shop in Regent street on the way to give an order about something being made there. I don't know what it was, or where the shop was situated, but at all events the three were walking abreast, the girls chattering and joking about the order. The sidewalk was very crowded, so that the mother stepped ahead, but heard her daughters' voices at her elbow for several minutes.

"The street grew clearer as she went, and she turned to beckon the girls alongside again. She didn't see them, and stood a few moments for them to catch up. After waiting awhile she walked back and still missed them. It occurred to her that they might have passed ahead without her noticing it, and gone on to the shop where they had planned to stop, so she went there and waited twenty minutes. Then she imagined they might have missed their way, and gone to the concert hall to wait for her. By this time she felt sufficient anxiety to hail a cab, but no one had seen them at the concert hall, and she herself had all three of the tickets, so she returned to their lodgings, sure that they would turn up there eventually in any case.

"At six o'clock they were still absent, and really frightened by this time she visited all the near-by police stations, but could get no news of them.

"That was four years ago, and from that day to this she has never seen or heard of them. She has travelled all over Europe and returned twice to America, has advertised in every possible way, and has employed the best detectives of both continents. Now she has come back for the third time, utterly broken in health and fortune. Their home in Philadelphia has become a boarding-house, and she has taken a room and will spend the rest of her life there, hoping that in that way, if they ever return, they may be able to reach her. Nearly all her money has gone in the search, and her mind is almost equally a wreck. She goes over to Philadelphia this afternoon, and I went in the morning to tell her good-by."

Mary said—her lips were white—"But, good heavens, Emily! where could the girls have gone?"

"That's the terrible part of it," Mrs. M—— answered. "One can't imagine. They were both so young. It was in a foreign country: they had no money. As far as the mother knew, neither had, nor could have had, any reason for going, nor anyone a reason for taking them. If one only had gone one might suspect a lover, or a sudden aberration of mind, but there were two; it was in broad daylight. Three minutes before they had been beside her. There was no struggle, no accident. No one could have silently carried off or made way with *two* grown girls in Regent Street in midday. One minute they were there, laughing, happy, and commonplace, and the next minute they had vanished utterly and forever, without a word or a cry."

"But why has one never heard of it?" I said.

"Well, of course, the mother kept it out of the papers. For a long time she feared they might have been the victims of the sort of person who preys on young girls, and dreaded that there should be a scandal by which their lives should be ruined if they ever returned. To-day I think she would be glad to find them even in the lowest brothel, if she might only see them again."

"Hadn't any of the police or detectives a theory?"

"Oh, thousands at first, but they never bore any fruit. Consider all the

29

circumstances. They were sensible, self-reliant American girls. By this time, if they were alive, they would have found some means of communicating with their mother. She has published guarded appeals, which they would understand, and always in the English language, in about every paper in this country and Europe."

"But what do you think?"

"What can one think? Can you conceive of any solution when you consider all the facts?"

"Has the mother no theory?"

"Well, she has, but then she is hardly sensible, you know, after the strain of such an experience. You've heard of the Fourth Dimension, haven't you? She says if that's not the explanation, she cannot imagine any other. She doesn't really believe it, I think, but she says if they did not stumble into it, where are they? And what answer can one give her?"

By this time it was late, and I came away. Outside the sun was shining and the trolley cars buzzing by. The theory of the Fourth Dimension seemed absurd, but I wondered where those poor young girls could have gone, and felt an oppression in my breathing.

JANUARY 23.
The Ant and the Lark.

Who, I wonder, was the stupid phrase-maker guilty of saying that Genius was only an infinite capacity for taking pains? And yet Shakespeare, according to tradition, never blotted a line. How much pains had the little Mozart taken when he began his first concert tour? Creation comes swiftly and with heat. The man who must take infinite pains in production is never a genius. Indeed, when one sees how little the creation of beauty, harmony, or ideas is related to their human creator, how little, in a way, he seems related to them, one is almost inclined to imagine that somewhere there exists a great reservoir of force and that the "genius" is merely a cock through which the creative fluid runs. He happens to be the cock that is "turned on" while the handles of the others are left untouched.

There was once a very ambitious and industrious Ant. Its home was in a field where the grass and flowers bloomed.

This Ant had convictions as to the best uses of life, and wasted no time. So many hours a day she devoted to the improvement of her mind, and so many to her life labour, which was to build an ant-hill. Early and late she toiled, and as she toiled she thought very deeply, elaborating numerous excellent and noble theories. All her theories concerned the best use of opportunities, and the doing of some work which should make the world better because she had existed.

Once in a long while, when quite worn out by her labours, she would climb to the top of a blade of grass, and look out into the world. Sometimes the sun was just rising and the field was damascened with the blue and white cups of morning-glories, and sometimes it was evening and the moon silvered the dew-hung grass, which palpitated with fireflies. At such times a divine yearning and great longing filled the heart of the tired little emmet, and she would hurry down to her work at once, saying bravely to herself:

"If I waste a moment my hill will never be high enough to look out upon this beautiful world." And so would toil on without ceasing, taking the greatest pains with every grain of sand, fitting and refitting it into its place with infinite pains, and comforting herself for her slow progress by saying:

"I am really not very old yet. I still have a great many days in which to complete my work." And would make some excuse to herself for going down to stand on the ground beside it and gain encouragement by noting how much greater was the hill than her own stature, and then went happily back to her task.

Near the Ant's hill a lark had built its home—a careless body, who roughly kicked out the earth for a nest, and who, being dull as she sat on her eggs, conversed at times with the Ant, for whom the matron manifested an ill-concealed contempt.

"In heaven's name!" she said, "What is the use of wearing yourself to skin and bone working on that hill? Isn't it quite big enough for your uses already?"

"Yes," replied the Ant, patiently, "but it is every one's duty to make the world as beautiful as they can, and I want to build the biggest and most beautiful ant-hill in the world. And oh!"—she cried, clasping her little paws and with a hungry look in her eyes—"I do so want to be famous!"

"Fiddle-de-dee!" answered the brown bird, contemptuously. "Famous!—what is that? Are you wearing yourself out for such nonsense? As for me, give me a fat worm for breakfast and luck with my eggs, and it's all I ask." Saying which, she tucked her head under her wing and went to sleep, while the Ant hurried away to finish the daily task she set herself.

In course of time a young lark was hatched. A great red, sprawling, featherless thing, with a big bill and no idea but worms. The Ant used to try sometimes, when his mother was absent hunting food, to teach the ugly young thing some of her own excellent theories, but the bird only blinked sleepily and scornfully and never answered a word, so the Ant was reluctantly obliged to give up the hope of ever inspiring him with the nobler ambitions of life.

She was growing much encouraged about her own work. All the other ants in the field wondered at and admired it, and as one could nearly see out above the grasses by standing upon her hill on tiptoe, the happy insect began to dream of immortality.

By this time, too, the young lark had grown feathers, and one morning he stumbled out of the nest, fluttered a moment to try his wings, and suddenly, bursting into a flood of song, soared upward into the sunlit blue.

The Ant fell to the earth, breathless and paralyzed, but in a moment, stifling her pain and despair, she rose up and began, from mere habit, fitting more grains of sand into her unfinished hill.

A Poet walked in the field that day, meditating some verses upon the divine gift of genius. He cried aloud with joy at the lark's song, and while he gazed upward stumbled over the Ant's hill and demolished it, but in his note-book he wrote:

"Oh, miracle of Genius, that lifts the Sons of God on golden pinions to the gates of heaven, while the dull myriads toil futilely at Babels below."

January 29.
The Döppelganger.

I suppose that everyone who has reached maturity has been aware of a sense of a dual personality—of a something within him that is a *me* and a *not me*; of opposing influences that puzzle his judgment, weaken his resolves, and warp his intention. These natures he finds engaged in an eternal conflict which sways him from the course he would instinctively follow, and draws him along lines of thought and conduct satisfying to neither side of his being, and achieving only a helpless compromise between the two.

"To be?"—"Or *not* to be?" contend the two at every crossing of the tangled meshes of existence, and neither disputant is ever convinced by the other's logic.

"To sleep"—says one. "Perchance to dream," replies the other coldly; and so gives pause to Hamlet's swift intentions.

Which is the real man? The Hamlet whose soul lusts for sudden brute revenge, whose promptings are the instinctive play of the natural man, or that frigid censor who checks the impulses of the first speaker and chills him with cold reasons and balancings of right and wrong, so that the sword falls from his nerveless hand at the very moment of opportunity? Or after all, is the real man the one whose actions are a continual endeavour to steer between the two promptings; the Hamlet whose doings are not in direct answer to either voice —are but furious and confused outbursts of indecision?

If it were at all possible to decide between the two, one would incline to think that the second voice, that chilling critic, was another self, alien to us, though entrenched in the very depths of the soul—was the *not me*, in everlasting opposition to the *me*—was the past warring with the present.

The warm, impulsive, blundering *me* we know, but who is that other? Whence comes this double, this *alter ego*, this bosom's lord, and strange, nameless ghost who haunts the house of life? How many thousand deaths have we died to give him life? For he is inexpressibly aged, infinitely sophisticated; and while the *me* still crowns its locks with youth's golden illusions, he is grey with knowledge and hoary with disenchantment. Though a part of our most intimate selves, he is not at one with us. He sympathizes with none of our enthusiasms, is tempted by none of our sins…. Sins!… what should he do eating forbidden fruit who is all compounded of the knowledge of good and evil?

"Ye shall be as gods, having eaten of that tree"—and like a god he sits in the dusk of the soul's seat, knowing the past, predicating the future, calmly beholding the fulfilling of our destiny. And yet is his grim wisdom of no avail, since—a shadowy Cassandra—he warns in vain. His deity-ship is of no more worth than that of the Olympian heavens, which might punish or reward, but could not divert the decrees of a power higher than itself. It is indeed the fate of all gods to have their creations caught from between their shaping hands by the blind, fumbling fingers with the shears. Gods may teach; may command; may ban or bless, but the being once made is Fate's creature, not theirs.

This cynical, impotent *döppelganger* goes by many names. His Christian cognomen is Conscience, and his voice is raised to exalt Christian tenets of clean living and high thinking.

"Thou shalt surely die," he declaims from the altar where he wears with cheerful indifference the livery of a faith in which he has no part, and we walk contentedly in the path he designates, flattering ourselves upon being upheld and guided by the voice of omnipotent truth, until passion trips our heels with some hidden snare, and, rolling headlong in the mire, we lift our stained faces in astonishment to behold that calm-lidded countenance all unstirred by our wild mishap. He foresaw, but he was helpless to prevent, nor does he greatly care, since he also knows that age after age every reincarnation of the spirit must be tempted anew by the ever-renewed, ever-lustful, unalterable flesh.

Weissman diverts himself and indulges the Teutonic weakness for word-building by naming this double self the "germ-plasm"—that immortal, eternal seed of life that links the generations in an unbroken chain; changing and developing only through the unreckonable processes of time, and taking heed not at all of the mere passing accidents of fleeting avatars.

Why should not this germ-plasm, this eternal ghost, be infinitely sophisticated? What surprises can its mere momentary envelope contrive for a consciousness as old as the moon? If temptations seduce the young flesh, though the old, old soul declares with scorn that teeth are set on edge by the eating of sour grapes, it is not surprised at all when the body persists in its will to seize upon the fruit of its desire, having seen in everyone of a myriad generations the same obstinacy and weakness of the flesh, which learns little and very hardly from the spirit.

Now and again—in his moments of exalted seriousness—man listens to this ancient voice of the spirit breathing the accumulated experience of time, and then it imposes upon him the ripened wisdom of its long retrospect of the generations, and man creates religions—by which he does not square his conduct—or philosophies—whose bit he immediately takes between his teeth.

But for the most part he stops his ears to the soul's stern, sad preaching with the thick wax of sentimentalism, and that undying determination that life shall be not what it is, but what he wishes it to be—and so stumbles along, through ever-renewed pangs and tragedies, after a mirage in the hard desert of existence, to whose stones and flints, despite his bruises, he will not turn his eyes. And well it is for us that upon many the mantle of flesh lies so warm and thick that this ghost called consciousness of self cannot chill their blood with his dank wisdom breathed from out a world of graves. In the hearts of such as these all the sweet illusions of existence came to full and natural bloom. To their lusty egoism life has all the exhilaration and freshness of a new and special creation.

Far otherwise is it with the haunted man, whose dwelling is blighted by that cold presence with its terrible memory. Forever echoes through his chambers the cry that hope will be unfulfilled, that love will die, the morning fade, that what has been will be again and forever again; that the waters of life will climb the shore only to crawl back again into the blind deeps of eternity; that the unit is forever lost in the eternal ebb and flux of matter. Endeavour can find no footing in this profundity of experience. To all desire, all aspiration, the ghost says in a paralyzing whisper:

"Scipio, remember that thou art a *man*—that everything has been done even if thou doest it not—that everything will be done whether thou doest it or no…. Where are the poems that were written in Baalbec? Where the pictures that were painted in Tadmor of the Wilderness? Are there fewer pictures and poems to-day because the men who made them are not? Who was prime minister to the bearded King of Babylon? Where is his fame?… Ay, drink this cup if you will, but you know well the taste of it is not good at the bottom. You have drunk it a thousand thousand of times, and the taste was never good, and yet you will drink it a thousand times again, hoping always that it will be good."…

And the haunted man sits with idle hands and withered purpose, listening always to the voice, while his neighbours push loudly on to die futilely but gloriously in the unending battle.

"An end-of-the-century disease," say these full-fed, happy egotists with lowered breath and eyes askance as they pass the haunted house. "The mould of age has fallen upon him and made him mad." Yet before the walls of Troy these two—the ghost-ridden, and the happy egotist—battled for the glowing shadow of a woman whom neither man loved nor desired. Achilles, blackly melancholy in his tent, heard the old voice cry

"ἐν δὲ ἰῇ τιμῇ ἠμὲν κακὸς ἠδὲ καὶ ἐσθλός"

and disdains the greatness of life and the littleness of it. To an iron inevitableness of fate he opposes only indifference and an unbending courage. That which has been will be, and the end is death and darkness. He has no illusions. He wars neither for love of country nor love of Helen. If Troy falls nothing is gained. If the Greeks fail nothing will be lost. In time all the sweat and blood shed upon Ilium's windy plain will evaporate into a mere mist of uncredited legend. In Achilles, the other self, the *alter ego*, is the stronger man. The ghost of dead experience is as living as he.

Not so is it with Hector. All the passions of humanity are as new and fresh to him as if none before himself had known them. He looks neither forward nor back. The present is his concern. What though men have died and been forgotten, he will not lessen his utmost effort, even to the giving up of his life to save Troy. That is to him the one thing of importance. So robust is his courage, his faith, his love, that the sad spirit of memory within him cannot speak loud enough to make him hear. There is no warring of dual personalities in him; he is aware of but one—that rich momentary incarnation called Hector, more potent than the memories and experiences of the thousands of lives that preceded him, that gave him existence.

What though Achilles was right; what though both be but dust and legend now—who would not choose that flash of being called Hector—Hector dragged at the chariot-heel of Achilles—Hector with wife enslaved and children slaughtered and his city's proud towers levelled with the plain, rather than to have been the haunted victor, triumphing but not triumphant; fighting without purpose or hope? The same end indeed came to both, but one died as he lived, for what he thought a glorious end, while the other too passed away —but with the cold knowledge that both deaths were fruitless and vain.

Troy is a dream, but the battle forever is waged between the fresh incarnation of being and the memories of past being. Every creature wakes out of childhood aware that he lives not alone in even the secretest chambers of his life. Which is the *I* he cannot always say. The two companions are never at one. Sometimes the struggle breaks into open flame. Sometimes the one is victor, sometimes the vanquished. Each fights for Helen, for his ideal of pleasure, of wisdom, or of good, but in the very handgrips of battle a chilling doubt will fall between them whether she for whom they war—call her virtue, beauty, lust, life, what you will—is the real Queen, or only some misleading eidolon whose true self is hid in distant Sparta; and so the grasp relaxes, the tense breath falls free, the selves mingle. Man gropes for truth and finds it vague, intangible, not to be grasped—a dream.

FEBRUARY 17.
"A Young Man's Fancy."

What is that ineffable quality in the air that says *Spring*?

Long ago, as far back as towards the end of January, there came suddenly one day a sense that the winter was conquered. There has been much cold weather since—we shall have much cold still, but there is always a promise in the air.

There is a sad day later in the year when one is aware all at once that summer is ending, and the warm, mild weeks that follow never console for that hour's realization that the apex is crossed and the rest of the path slopes downward. Just such a day comes in one's life,—while one is still young and strong—a sudden sense that youth is done; the climacteric of passion passed. Life has a long Indian summer still, but it's never again the real thing,—that ripening toward fruition; that ecstasy of expansion and growth. There is no visible change for a while, yet every day there is an imperceptible fall in the temperature. Always the nights are growing longer. The flowers drop away one by one—the sap sinks a little, leaving the extreme delicate twigs moribund. No one has seen the leaves fall, yet there are fewer upon the bough —winter is coming.

Age is peaceful, perhaps—but middle age—! The wave clings to the shore, but the inexorable ebb draws it down relentlessly into the deep. This is the time that men go *musth*, like old elephants. This is the period when both men and women do their mad deeds, which belie all their previous records. It is their one last frantic clutch after vanishing romance and passion. Men buy a semblance of it from young women sometimes, and resolutely endeavour to persuade themselves that it is the real thing—that gold can renew youth, can purchase a second summer—but they know well that it is only a mechanical imitation. Those cruel old satirists, the comedy writers, loved to paint the trembling dotard resolutely shutting his eyes to the lusty young rival hiding behind the jade's petticoats.

As for the women!—who shall tell the real story of the middle age of women? —of the confident coquette, who one day turns away to punish her slave, and finds, when she relents, that his eyes are fixed upon her daughter?—of the bewildered inspection of the mirror, that still tells a fluttering tale of curves and colours, though startled experience shows the eyes of men turning in preference to crude, red-elbowed girls, obviously her inferior in grace and charm?—of the shock of finding that the world is no longer much interested in her—the amazement of the discovery that the handsome lads see little difference between a woman of thirty-five and one of fifty?—of the shame-faced misery of learning that the passion, which she has virtuously resolved to repulse, is given in reality to her niece? Her charm, her sweetness, her well-preserved beauty is as nothing beside mere raw youth. Undeveloped figures, flat chests, blotchy complexions, are of more value than her rounded mellow loveliness. She is pushed from her throne by giggling girls, who stare at her in hard contempt and wonder openly what the old creature does lingering belated in this galley.

Though she be called "a fine woman" still, men of all ages will turn from her to dote upon an empty-headed debutante. Her comprehension and sympathy, her wit and her learning are less enthralling than the vapid babblings of red-cheeked misses just out of pinafores. Her heart is as young as ever; she knows herself capable of a finer, nobler passion and tenderness than the girl can dream of, yet the selfish, egotistic emotions of the self-confident chit awake a rapture that would be dulled by the richest warmth she could give.

"Age, I do abhor thee:
Youth, I do adore thee;
O, my love, my love is *young!*"

That she in her turn elbowed the preceding generation from its place comforts her not at all. Oh, for again one hour only of the splendid domination of youth —one rich instant of the power to intoxicate!…

There is nothing for it but to keep such things to one's self, and jog on quietly and respectably to the end. One has had one's turn.

That mad girl Spring has passed up this way
    With a hole in her pockets,
For here lies her money all strewn in the grass—
    Broad dandelion ducats.

She'll be needing this wealth ere the end of the year
    For a warm winter gown,
Though now she's content with a breast-knot of buds
    And a violet crown.

She heard in the green blooming depths of the wood
    The voice of a dove,
And she dropped all these flowering coins as she ran
    To meet summer and love.

'Twill not serve you to gather from out her wildpath
    All your two hands can hold—
Only youth and the Spring may buy kisses and mirth
    With this frail fairy gold.

FEBRUARY 18.
An Arabian Looking-glass.

There has been great recrudescence of the Essay of late—none of it very important, I take the liberty of thinking. We moderns have lost the trick of it. All of us, at least, but Stevenson, and he hardly seems a modern, so closely is he related to the great classics, with his inheritance of the Grand Style, like the *bel canto*, now a lost art. And yet the Essay is a great temptation. Doubtless not one of all those who go down into the ink-bottle with pens has quite escaped its seduction. Generally it is, I suspect, merely an outcropping of the somewhat too widely known need of the artistic nature for "self-expression" in more definite terms than ordinary work permits.

The young fellows, still walking in the light of the eternal pulchritudes, are touchingly anxious lest they "falsify themselves"—pathetically unaware of the supreme unconcern of the rest of humanity as to their personal veracity. The line between art and the other thing is drawn just across this zone of egotism. "The other thing" is a man's expression of himself; Art is the mirror in which each observer sees only his own face. The Arabian legend of the prosperous old beggar who, making a pilgrimage to Mecca, left to his son, as his sole means of support, a looking-glass, and returned to find the boy starving and gazing into the mirror himself, is supposed to cynically suggest the uses of judicious flattery, but has deeper application. Speak of yourself—the world yawns. Talk to it of itself—rudely, vaguely, profoundly, how you will—and it hangs upon your lips. Turn the mirror toward it and it says proudly, "Of just such exalted devotion and sacrifice am I capable," or mutters with a shudder, "There, but for the grace of God, goes Augustine."

The tenor sings *"Sous ta Fenetre"* and every face is lighted by the inner shining of romance. The strangest revelations are discerned upon the countenances of respectable matrons, of rangé men of affairs. They beat their hands together in a flooding wave of applause, and the greasy Italian in his uneasy evening dress swells with a strutting consciousness of his vocal chords, of his method, his upper C, of his own value.

O tempora! O mores! He is nothing whatever to them. It is only that in every human heart there is a chord that vibrates to C in alt. They are quite unaware of him, and of his greasy personality. Every man is singing with his own soul's voice under the lattice of his first beloved. Every woman is leaning to listen to a dream lover yearning up to her through the warm scented moonlight. As for the garlicky loves of the singer they care not one jot whether he loves or not. It is all a question of themselves, of a vibration.

MARCH 4.
The Cry of the Women.

I have been clearing out a lot of old books, preparatory to moving, and have been amused to see how empty and dead many already are, which a few years since were raging through edition after edition, and were the subject of so much talk and interest. Already more than half have grown as desiccated and unimportant as last year's leaves, and their "timeliness" seems of a time as far past as the deluge. There was among these dead books a group on the Woman Question, which already, in so short a space, has lost all its interrogation point. Is it that there was really no Woman Question, or has the Question already received an answer?

Usually one is inclined to think that when a book voices with truth and passion the needs and thoughts of even a portion of humanity, it has a real claim to be classed as literature, though it fails of the immortality which is the meed only of such writings as express with beautiful verity the immortal, unchanging needs of life. But already one regards with amused indifference yesterday's crop of novels written by women, with their vague ecstasies of longing, their confused cries of discontent, their indistinct moans and reproaches, though such a very short time since those books faithfully expressed the mental state of the sex, as one could not doubt, seeing the greediness with which editions were called for of "The Heavenly Twins," "Keynotes," "A Superfluous Woman," and their like, or listening to the echoes awaked by their inchoate sentiments in the feminine mind. Yet the sum of the protest of all these books by women was like the cry of an infant—suffering but inarticulate.

I suppose the truth is that even so short a time since free thought and free speech were still so new to women that, struggling in the swaddling bands of ignorance and convention, it was small wonder that she could not state with precision, or even define clearly to herself, where her pain lay, nor how she would allay it. She knew she was in revolt against what had been. She could not yet choose what she would change in the future. Some of them cried out for larger political rights, others were convinced that the abolition of stays and the introduction of trousers was all that was needed to produce a feminine millennium.

"Latch-keys!" cried the browbeaten English girls—"and freedom to be out after dark like our own brothers. Look at the men. They are quite happy. It must be the possession of latch-keys that makes them so: give them also to us."

"No," roundly declared a certain Mona Caird, "what we really need is a latch-key to let us out of the lifelong oppressive bond of marriage. It weighs too heavily upon us—let us go free!"

"Nonsense!" contradicted Sarah Grand. "Marriage is all right. What is wrong is man. He comes to the marriage altar with stained and empty hands, while he demands that ours be spotless, and heaped with youth, health, innocence, and faith. He swindles us. Reform man if you would make us happy!"

"Higher education"—"Equal wages"—"Physical development"—"No household drudgery"—"Expansion of the ego," cried the conflicting voices; each with a quack panacea for the disease of discontent.

Can it be that all this was but ten years ago? How quickly ideas are changing!

I think that this noise among the women was the last wave of the democratic ideal expending itself. It was their restlessness under a sense of their inferiority to man. Until the nineteenth century, woman had been content to accept the male of her kind, with his mental and physical endowments, as the true standard of human excellence, and to humbly admit that she permanently failed to reach that standard.

The universality of the democratic ideal aroused in her at last an unwillingness to admit her innate inferiority, and drove her to a desperate search for some fountain of Salmacis that should transmute her to an exact likeness of her long-time lord and superior. The search, of course, was delayed and confused by that furious and debasing *fin de siecle* demand for happiness at all cost. She heard no talk anywhere of courage, submission, or duty. The later decades of the democratic century had refused to contemplate the world-old riddle of the blind Fates who create one vessel to honour and another to dishonour. So woman, no more than her fellows, would consider the caprices of destiny which from the union of one man and one woman will produce an heir to beauty, talent, and success, and from the same union— without volition or intention upon anyone's part—brings forth a cripple, an idiot, or the helpless Inadequate, who is foredoomed to failure with a grim gravitation no human laws or institutions can arrest. The nineteenth century was a sentimental one; unwilling to consider unpleasant truths. "All men *are* born equal," it stubbornly persisted in asserting, and then was rather shocked when some of its offspring sought this equality of happiness at the sword's point or the bomb's fuse—as if content was a coin to be stolen and concealed about the person of the thief.

Of course, the women finally became infected with the bacillus of unsound ideas, and struggling against the immutable burden of sex ran to and fro, crying "Lo, here!" and "Lo, there!" and wailing, "Where is *my* happiness? Who has my happiness? You men have stolen and are keeping it from me!"

A certain part of the charge was true, too. Men had filched from her.

The theft was not a new one. If the statute of limitations could ever run in crimes against nature it might have almost ceased to be a wrong in this case, after the lapse of nearly two thousand years.

Morgan in his "Ancient Society," dealing with the question of *Mütter-Recht*, declares that throughout the earliest period of human existence regarding which any knowledge is attainable, descent and all rights of succession were traced through the women of the *gens* or clans, into which primitive man was organized. Women, as being the bearers and protectors of the young, were regarded as the natural land owners, and therefore did not leave their homes to follow the fathers of their children, lest they should lose their own possessions and rights of inheritance. Instead, the men married into the sept of their wives. The power and independence of women was lost at last through the practice of making female captives in war. These had no land and were the property of, and dependent upon the will of, their male captor. In course of time men naturally grew to prefer these subservient wives. The Arab advises his son: "It is better to have a wife with no claims of kin and no brethren near to take her part."

Women therefore began to dread capture as the greatest of evils. After the movements of vast hordes began—the marches of the race columns across the continents—with their wars of spoliation and conquest, there was no security save in physical strength, and the females yielded all claims to the men in return for protection. It was better, they thought, to be a slave at home than a slave among strangers. Still the man, while asserting physical superiority, claimed none morally. Under the pagan rule of Rome, the jurisconsults, by their theory of "Natural Law," evidently assumed the equality of the sexes as a principle of their code of equity. Sir Henry Maine says there came a time "when the situation of the female, married or unmarried, became one of great personal and proprietary independence; for the tendency of the later law ... was to reduce the power of the guardian to a nullity, while the form of marriage conferred on the husband no compensating superiority."

Among the Germanic races of the Roman period, a woman was occasionally ruler of the tribe, and the blue-eyed wife of the roving Barbarian, as well as the proud Roman matron, were held alike in high esteem for their functions as wife and mother. The priestess crowned with oak leaves, officiating at the sylvan altars of the forest, or the Vestal Virgin serving the fires of the white temples of Rome, were alike held worthy of speaking face to face with the gods and of conveying their blessings to man. It was the humble religion of

Judea—which women embraced with ardour, and to which they were early and willing martyrs—that cursed them with a deadly curse. It denied woman not only mental and physical, but moral equality with man, and besmirched the very fountain and purpose of her being with a shameful stain. It made her presence in the most holy places a desecration, and for the first time regarded her feminine functions as a disgrace rather than a glory. And this although the founder of the Christian faith had set an example of reverence and tenderness for the sex in his own life, and had left his mother to be raised to a heavenly throne by his worshippers. Never from his lips had fallen a word that could give warrant for the insult offered woman by his church. He was the first of all men living to denounce the injustice of visiting upon the woman the whole penalty of a double sin, and his life was beautified with the tenderest friendships with women. But already, before a church had been fairly organized, Paul was dictating silence to women, covered heads and supreme submission to the male, and was declaring against marriage as a weakness. If a man must marry because of his weakness, he might do so, but not to marry was better.

Scorn of woman and her functions grew. Antagonism to marriage intensified. Woman by the very law of her existence was a curse and a temptation to sin. Hear Tertullian—one of the fathers of the Church—on this subject:

"Do you not know that each one of you is an Eve? The sentence of God on this sex of yours lives in this age; the guilt must of necessity live too. You are the devil's gateway; you are the unsealer of the forbidden tree; you are the first deserter of the divine law; you are she who persuaded him who the devil was not valiant enough to attack. You destroyed so easily God's image, man. On account of your desert—that is death—the Son of God had to die!"

This is but one of a thousand similar insults by the early writers of the Church —all Patristic books bristle with them.

Lecky, comparing the Roman jurisprudence with the canon or ecclesiastical law, remarks that "the Pagan laws during the earlier centuries of the Empire were constantly repealing the disabilities of women, whereas it was the aim of the canon law to substitute enactments which should impose upon the female sex the most offensive personal restrictions and stringent subordination."

Even marriage and the production of offspring—which in the pagan world had been an honour to both sexes—was stigmatized. No priest of God might approach a woman, scarcely even look at her, and no woman was allowed to serve at God's altar. Celibacy was a virtue so great in man that none set apart for the highest duties might marry, and woman was encouraged to suppress in herself all the sweet and wholesome instincts for motherhood—an instinct upon which the race hung dependent, one for which she willingly suffered the sharp pangs of childbirth—and instead to immure herself in convents and endeavour to find solace in the spiritual ecstasies of morbid meditation.

Now was woman at last robbed and poor indeed! Her social and civil equality having been yielded in exchange for protection, her protectors had bereft her of all moral rights, and denounced as unclean the function for the perfect performance of which she had paid out all her goods. It was the triumph of the Oriental idea over the ideals of the Occident, and so deeply did the Eastern thought stamp itself upon the Western mind that only to-day the latter begins to free itself from the yoke of the Asian Paul's fierce egotism of sex. So deeply indeed did this thought penetrate, that historians do not hesitate to attribute to this scorn of woman and her mission of childbearing a long delay in the development of European civilization. The higher spiritual natures, being more under the influence of the Church, accepted its suggestions of asceticism and left the baser sort to perpetuate the race and thus delayed the processes of evolution.

It was the denial by the Church of the beauty and nobility of natural love that drove the Middle Ages to the invention of chivalry and the romantic love of the unwedded, that they might evade the ban and find some outlet for the emotions.

With the Reformation, that first uprising of the Western mind against Asian domination, men threw off the yoke in so far as it bound their own necks, and declared the rightness and reasonableness of all their mental and physical functions. It was no longer a shame for the priest of God to mate with a woman, nor a weakness for a man to round his life with the fulness of joy to be found in connubial love, when he at the same time assumed its duties and responsibilities. The ingrained contempt of women was not so easily eradicated. Honour the man defined for himself as integrity, *wholeness*, a development of every power to its highest possibility. Honour for woman was simply chastity. That is to say, if she repressed all the animal side of life she might entirely neglect the spiritual. She might be but indifferently honest, a liar, a slanderer and a tattler, guilty of every minor baseness, and yet be held in good and honourable repute. The wonder is that woman's morals survived at all so false a training!

Centuries of such teaching wrought their wretched work despite all the forces of nature. Virginity instead of purity became the ideal of the highest type of woman, who shrank from the fulfilment of her functions as a stepping down, instead of glorying in it as the fulfilment of her sacred purpose. What had been urged upon her upon every side she endeavoured to conform to in the spirit as well as the letter. Her mind strained towards the virginal as well as her body. The higher type of woman cried out to man for spiritual rather than

47

physical love, and she found his natural sane tenderness for her person brutal rather than beautiful. The young girl, sedulously guarded from knowledge of the fundamental reasons of her being, cast suddenly and unprepared into marriage, shrank with disgust from a relation which her husband—educated in wholeness of thought—regarded as the culmination of the flower of life into its fruit. It is not too much to say that four fifths of all modest, pure girls —as a result of their foolish training—contemplated the sexual relation with the bitterest reluctance. They had been led to believe that virginity was in itself a virtue, instead of regarding it only as the sanctification of the body until such time as it legitimately becomes the temple of life. With many this feeling survived marriage, and embittered it to both the wife, who resented what she looked upon as a baser nature in the man, and to the man who resented, and was rebuffed by the coldness of his companion.

At least half of the disappointments and failures of marriage arose from the mistaken training of good women.

Ten years ago this Patristic ideal still had a strong hold upon the race, but the long centuries of study of the Latin and Greek literatures in the schools finally, almost suddenly, bore fruit. We had through our school boys and girls imbibed the spirit of the two European races whom the Semitic influences had never dominated. One wonders that some foolish so-called progressives should now be wishing to drop those literatures from the curriculum of students, though perhaps their work is done. At all events we hear very little now of this talk of the inferiority of women.

When the miracles of male achievement are pointed to to-day, women know enough to say proudly, "Did man make this? Well, I made man"; and is content.

MAY 4. SEVILLE.
The Beauty of Cruelty.

What a people are these,—these Spaniards! This afternoon—Sunday—I saw my first bull-fight. One need never wonder again at the Roman Arena and its horrors. It is as incredible that human beings can sit through such spectacles as that women could have reversed their thumbs when a staggering, bloody barbarian turned up a glazed eye to seek mercy.... And this, after two thousand years of Catholicism, of Christianity!

These Spaniards say—staring stupidly at your horror—"Mas, no es Cristianos. They are only animals." Animals!—and yet Christians dare talk of divine mercy; of their faith having softened hearts, and sweetened human nature. Civilization has done so, in truth, but where this faith reigns most arbitrarily such an atrocious spectacle is permissible; goes undenounced of its priests.

It is not the baser sort alone who love this cowardly butchery. In the same box with ourselves sat a woman and her two daughters, evidently members of the upper classes. The arena below was crowded with the people—women in sulphur-coloured shawls, embroidered with sharp blues and scarlets—men of all classes—dandies and workmen cheek by jowl—but the rows of boxes above held the women and children of the well-to-do, even the aristocracy. The Royal family itself patronizes the arena.

The women, whose faces I watched instead of the shambles after the fight began, grew devilish, a hard smile drew their lips back over their teeth; their eyes glittered; a look of lust strained the lines about the nose. They forced the children—some of whom cried, and shrank from the horrid sight—to turn and see the blood and the struggle.

I believe the secret charm of this gory game to many is the prick that the sight of blood gives to the senses. The history of war is full of evidence of this fact —that the sight of horrors spurs the passions. It was curious to think that many of the people there owed their existence to just such a stimulus as this. Cruelty thus lies, hereditarily, at the very roots of their being; intensified in each generation.

For the same reason, I suppose, that so much of my life seems to me a glamour of tangled shadows, elusive and shifting, with no definite line between the real and the unreal, between to-day and all the yesterdays—for that reason the arena's gaunt, windowless walls and passages seemed startlingly familiar. Equally familiar the yellow, sand-strewn circle; the glaring blue sky above the bright-coloured maelström of faces; the whirl of fans all around the ring—as of a circle of innumerable dancing butterflies; the cries of the venders; the clang of the trumpets; the glitter of the tinsel and gew-gaws; the bold rush of the black bull; the quick spatter of the applauding hands....

No animal was ever more beautiful than this splendid beast, the perfect focus of power and rage. He knew that he was facing murder. There was desperation in his glance from the first moment, but he simply didn't know the meaning of cowardice. He knew there was no use in anything he might do; that his courage, and beauty, and long battle for life, would not stir to pity one of those hard, handsome faces with their dark shaven jaws and tight lips, but he struck at his foes with all his force in mere sullen fury. He tore open the bellies of the shivering, sweating, blindfolded horses, who staggered a few steps trailing their entrails in the sand and then crumpled helplessly; he caught a man in the breast and tossed him over the barrier with blood spurting from the hole his horn had made. He himself leaped the fence once, as agile as a deer, and brushed the crowd back like flies, but he did it all without a sign of hope, and *never made a sound.*

Pricked, goaded, red streams running over his satin skin and searing his eyes, stumbling wildly here and there, his sides sunk in, his muzzle dragging in the dust, dumb, dull fury in his heart at his useless torture, spurred to new effort by explosive darts that tore his flesh into gory, pendulous ribbons, hissed by the women, he fell at last upon his knees in blind helplessness....

How it ended I don't know. A rage of horror squeezed my heart till the tears spurted from my lids. It seemed necessary to seize some weapon and slaughter indiscriminately the men who were murdering this poor brute for mere amusement, the women who were hissing his death throes. In such horrid sequence does cruelty engender cruelty.

The people about me regarded my emotion and retreat with surprise and contempt. Some such sensation, I suppose, as would have been felt by a Roman who should have seen me shed tears when the big cats of the arena crushed the bones of some brave young barbarian or Christian. These creatures were so far beneath him in the scale of existence that he could not conceive of any poignancy of suffering or emotion in such a mere animal. Was not one hair of a Roman worth many sparrows—or Christians?

The Jewish democrat tried to teach the world to recognize the value of the individual, the sanctity of each human life—when will a Christ of the beasts arise?

May 5.

This old world, with its horrors and its beauties, how tame it makes our smug, comfortable America appear!... Yesterday I wished to make a hecatomb of the Spaniards. To-day I forgive them everything because of the Sevillian dancers. My lusts are all of the eye. I can quite conceive Herod tossing the Baptist's head to the supple Salome in an ecstasy of approval. Dancing, when it is good, is more beautiful to me than music. And this dancing is very good.

The muscular gymnastics, which modern Italy has imposed upon the world as dancing, are as dissimilar from the real thing as the fiorituri singing is from the old bel canto. The Spaniards make dancing—as all arts should be made— the poetical expression of life and love. Such ardour and seduction, such abandon to the joy of living, such rage and daring, such delicate coquetry and wild wooing!... there is nothing like it out of Spain, the country where they torture helpless animals for sport.

Is there, perhaps, some secret tie between cruelty and beauty; between crime and art? It is certain that religious reformers have always thought so, and have acted with logical fury. In our peaceful, decent country, beauty, except such as Nature herself affords, is rare. A race that loves its neighbour as itself seems incapable of creating an art. The good Swiss have done nothing for the mind's delight: the virtuous Spartans could not even appreciate loveliness when they saw it. Nearly all the great periods of flowering in art come after the roots of a nation have been watered in blood, after some frightful *crise* of suffering. It would seem as if bringing forth must be always accompanied by birth-pangs.

MAY 7. GRANADA.
The Duke of Wellington's Trees.

H—— said that the greatness of a people depended upon its trees. This sounded rather cryptic, and I entreated him to be more diffuse. We were walking home from that enchanted garden, owned by the Pallavicini, which rewarded the Moor for betraying his city. The May moon was shining on the white mountain tops, and the jargoning of the snow-brooks sounded about our feet. The air smelled of orange flowers and roses, and the nightingales were *shouting* in the gloom of those one hundred thousand trees planted by the Duke of Wellington.

"This Spanish peninsula," H—— said, "under the rule of the Moors, supported thirty millions of people in comfort. The Christian kings allowed the upland forests to be ruthlessly sacrificed, and now look at Spain."

"One swallow"—I quoted. "Will one instance support a theory?"

"No; but I could give you a dozen. Carlyle and the rest of the historians have talked the fearfulest rot about France under the monarchy which preserved her forests. Of course, every one has weakly credited the stories of oppression and starvation in aristocratic France. And yet the sons of these peasants, who were pitifully pictured snatching at leaves of those forests for food, overran Europe. I don't believe that children bred in starvation could ever have had the vitality to be conquerors. At all events, when the land was divided and the forests delivered to spoliation, the population of France began to decline. Possibly the modern effort at reforesting the country may arrest that decline."

"Just listen to the noise of those nightingales," I said. "Do you suppose we shall be able to sleep?"

MAY 15. NAPLES.
The Boy with the Goose.

The Pompeian bronze, which the guide books and catalogues name The Boy with the Goose, is quite wrongly named. The lad carries a wine-skin. The rude, swollen outlines of the pig are clear, and the attitude of the boy one may see any water-seller in Tangier assume when called upon for a drink—the arm raised, the body tilted back upon the hip to elevate the lip of the skin, so that no more water may flow than is needed. The whole, a delicious bit of *genre*, smiling and vivid after two thousand years.

There is a curious vitality of a trifling custom discoverable here in the Pompeian museum. The great bronze horses of Balbo have forelocks wrapped and twisted in exactly the same fashion that still prevails all along this Neapolitan shore. The breed has changed utterly; bone and structure have altered and shrunk, but the vetturino, who drives through the streets of Naples to-day, twists up that bit of hair in exactly the same manner as did the coachman of Glaucus or Balbo.

MAY 30. ROME.
A God Indeed.

How beautiful upon the mountains are the feet of—Apollo!... I have to-day, for the first time, seen a god.

He stands in the Vatican, and follows, with upthrown head and far-seeing eye, the flight of the golden arrow that slays the serpent of the miasmatic marsh. One feels a sad tenderness for the poor bleeding deity, who hangs dead and helpless from a thousand crucifixes here in Rome, but to-day, for the first time in my life, I felt the impulse to fall on my knees and worship. Here is at last, and indeed a god, whose fine feet disdain the earth, whose proud youth never knew suffering or defeat. Here is the embodiment of the ideal of the European —beauty, health, power. How he must smile to stand here, merely a statue, in the place where the Christian reigns, amid luxury and pomp, in the name of the sorrowful Hebrew democrat who had not a place to lay his head. Apollo's ideal, his worship, still remains dominant, though they call his religion by another name. The European remains, and always will remain, a pagan; none more pagan than the popes with their lust for temporal power.

Only here in Rome is it possible to realize the long struggle for supremacy between the European and Semitic ideas; for here is gathered the bulk of the relics of Greece—mother and nurse of our race—who early broke the bonds of Asiatic thought and sought her own development, material rather than spiritual (if one accepts the theory that spirit and matter are divisible), sensuous rather than mystical, concerned more with the well-being of the body and the freedom and vigour of the mind than with the condition of the soul. She who threw herself with passion into the arms of Nature, and worshipped only the sublimated human characteristics and visible natural forces deified into exquisite personifications. She who exalted the beauty and health of the body into a cult, strove after the demonstrable truths of science, and loved man as he was—humorously loved him with all his faults and limitations, rather than an impossible ideal of him.

Here in Rome one finds all the records of the next great development of the European Erd-geist—the growth of its genius in military, social, and political organization. Still, as in Greece, clinging to the aristocratic ideal; to the rule of the strong and gifted. The fruit did not exist for the benefit of the vine; the vine existed to produce, to nourish, to minister to the perfect culmination of its species in the fruit, which drank its sap as of right. Here again the European followed Nature, that Arch-Aristocrat who destroys multitudes to produce a few perfect specimens—whose right is always might.

The Asian conquests brought again inroads of Asian thought; more particularly the thought of that small tribe, the quintessential of Semitism, which was ever engaged in revolt against nature, and maintaining democratic convictions in the teeth of all experience. Impatient of rulers, but submissive to those who scourged the impulses of their appetites. Scornful of kings, and turning from beauty and genius to exalt the insane and insect-ridden fakir with knotted unshorn locks who muttered vague prophecies. Struggling always to escape from the grip of the inevitable cruelties of natural forces by opposing to them bloody sacrifices and cruel self-restraints—flowering at last into that supreme incarnation of the Semitic mind called Jesus Christ, who wrested from asceticism a dream of a panacea for the brutalities of the laws of life. The misshapen and undeveloped fruit of the tree of existence, the windfalls—always a vast majority—received with ecstasy this new gospel, absurd but fascinating, which denied actualities and promised impossibilities. The feeble majority clutched at a power denied them by nature, and only by outwardly accepting the new tenets were the strong few able to maintain their old dominance.

Nietsche's "blond savage" pouring in from the north found Rome disintegrated by this Asian influence, and unable to discern that the new faith was not an integral part of the civilization whose splendour dazzled him, accepted this theory of life as part of the lesson he set himself humbly to learn at the feet of Italy.

Hence followed that blind welter of mediævalism; the material genius of the European race struggling in the bonds of a creed entirely foreign and unsympathetic. The strong still ruled, as always, but ruled by new formulæ, and moistened with blood and kneaded by swords the hard paste of the European Aryan was leavened by Semitism. Not willingly; never entirely. A thousand years after Rome's acceptance of the new cult the re-discovery of the old art and philosophy of Greece intoxicated Europe with joy. Here was something of her own—natural to her—sympathetic. The Renaissance became an ecstasy of negation of the heavy yoke under which her neck had so long been bowed. Learning again was glorious. The philosopher dared assert his superiority to dirty, ignorant scions of the gutter, who had claimed equality with sovereigns by reason of not eating three meals a day, and because of the virtue which lay in the frequent recitation of gibberish. Art abandoned its endless repetitions of a single theme, and essayed in faltering delight to rival the glorious fragments of those who had made nature their model and had joyed to picture life in all its rich grace and charm. The Western world stood once more upon its feet and burst into a rapture of creation. It laughed to scorn the narrow commands of Semitic asceticism against the graven image. Once more it allowed the beauty of visible nature to pour through its veins in a rich, fecundating flood.

But after all, the leaven had reached every part, and had tinctured it past any possible casting out. Never could the European be free of Asian influence. The pendulum has swung back and forth ever since—ever moving a little higher toward the side of the natural, material development of the race, but ever checked and brought back to the old Jewish revolt against nature. To-day the influence of Asia shows itself in the absurdities of democracy, the phantasies of socialism.

… One of the most curious phases of the whole question is that the Jew— dispersed throughout the Western world—has entirely succumbed to the very ideas which he overthrew. He is the artist, the materialist of our times!

JUNE 1.
A Question of Skulls.

The portrait busts of the Romans were their highest achievements in art. One sees literally thousands of them in Italy, and their painstaking accuracy is obvious. What is to me most interesting is that the sculptured Roman head and face might easily be taken for a portrait of the English people of to-day. In any congregation of the English governing classes will be found constantly reproduced the long, narrow skull, the bold aquiline nose, the stern lips and chin, and that clean fleshless outline of the Roman—resembling the keen modelling of the head of the high-bred horse—repeated so frequently in marble and porphyry in all these museums.

Can it be that Empire reproduces the type? Yet ethnologists trust more to the shape of the skull in the study of race affinities than to any other proof. The modern Italian skull is the extreme opposite in type; is short and broad; so indeed is the skull of all the continental races of Europe. I know that the skull measurements are not supposed to give this result, but to the eye the English alone seem to possess this long, narrow skull.

Amusing also is it to remark that the Roman women were not handsome. In both races the resemblance between the sexes is too strong. The fine, bony, equine type, so admirable in the male Roman and Englishman, becomes hardness in the women, who lack seduction and charm. Also curious to note, there is the same proud grace of costume and coiffure in the men; the same ugliness and lack of taste in the arrangement of the hair and dress of the women of the two races.

LONDON. JUNE 30.
The Modern Woman and Marriage.

H—— and I dined last night with Mary L—— at the Carleton, and H——
asked her, in his large generic fashion, what everybody had been doing at
home during our absence.

"Oh, having their appendices cut out and getting divorced!" she said
flippantly, and H—— laughed outrageously, so that people turned and stared.
It was probably the lobster we ate that made me think her remark more
pathetic than funny while I turned it over in my mind all the long hours I lay
awake.

Howells has said, with only humorous apology, that his sex, after nineteen
hundred years, is but imperfectly monogamous, and yet our modern women
are beginning to treat marriage so disrespectfully, and change partners for life
as light-heartedly as if the engagement was as unimportant as an engagement
for a dance!

That even this imperfect measure of self-denial and fidelity has been arrived
at by men seems to me to be almost solely due to the women of the past. I
know the Church claims—in her usual arrogant way—that she should have
the credit of it, but Lecky says in his "European Morals":

"The first consequence of the prominence of asceticism was a profound
discredit thrown upon the domestic virtues. The extent to which this discredit
was carried, the intense hardness of heart and ingratitude manifested by the
saints towards those who were bound to them by the closest of earthly ties, is
known to few who have not studied the original literature on the subject.
These things are commonly thrown into the shade by sentimentalists who
delight in idealizing the devotees of the past. To break by his ingratitude the
heart of the mother who had borne him, to persuade the wife who adored him
that it was her duty to separate from him for ever, to abandon his children,
uncared for and beggars, to the mercies of the world, was regarded by the true
hermit as the most acceptable offering he could make to his God."

The root of family life is not mutual affection between man and woman,
because that, alas!—whether it be founded on physical attraction or mental
affinity—is subject to change. Age withers, and custom stales it: circumstance
blights it, a diversity of spiritual growth rends it apart, and no man or woman
can say with certainty that it will endure for a lifetime. But the fluctuations to
which wedded love is subject are unknown to the self-abnegating instinct of

parenthood. Mutual affection for the offspring will hold together the most opposite natures; it will rivet for all existence two lives that must otherwise inevitably spring asunder by instinctive repulsion.

Love of offspring is in man a cultivated emotion; in woman an instinct. There are women lacking the instinct as there are calves born with two heads, but for purposes of generalization these exceptions may be ignored. In many of the lower orders of life the female is obliged to protect the young from the enmity of the male parent. The alligator finds no meal so refreshing as a light lunch off his newly hatched children, and the male swine shares this epicurean taste for tender offspring. The stallion is a dangerous companion for the mare with colt at foot, though the colt be of his own get, and many species of male appear to experience a similar jealousy of the young while absorbing the attentions of the female. Speaking generally of the animal world, the young are obliged to look to the mother entirely for food and care during the period of helplessness. With savage man of the lower grade the paternal instinct is still faint and rudimentary, and even where the woman has, through long ages of endeavour, succeeded in cultivating in the heart of the other parent a fair imitation of her own affection, this affection, being a cultivated emotion and not an instinct, frequently breaks down under stress of misbehaviour or frowardness on the part of the child.

To this end, then,—that end "toward which the whole creation moves,"—to effect this result of an equal care and affection for the offspring, all the energies of women have been bent for ages.

She has fought polygamy with incessant hatred; not only for its injury to herself, but its constant menace to her children. The secret strings of the woman's heart are wrapped about the fruit of her own flesh, but the desire of the man is to the woman, and this desire she has used as a lever to work her will—not consciously, perhaps, not with reasoned forethought, but with the iron tenacity of blind instinct. Reasoned will may be baffled or deflected, but water can by no means be induced to run up hill; and so while woman has been apparently as fluidly yielding as water—to be led here and driven there according to the will of her master—she has stuck to her own ends with a silent persistency that has always tired out opposition at last. She has, like Charity, suffered all things, endured all things; she has been all things to all men. She has yielded all outward show of authority; she has submitted to be scoffed at as an inferior creation, to be sneered at for feebleness and shallow-mindedness, to be laughed at for chattering inconsequence, and to be regarded as a toy and trifle to amuse man's leisure hours, or as a dull drudge for his convenience, for ends are not achieved by talking about them. All the ages of masculine discussion of the Eternal Feminine show no reply from her, but to-day the world is a woman's world. Civilization has, under the unrelaxing pressure of endless generations of her persistent will, been bent to her ends. Polygamy is routed, and the errant fancy of the male tamed to yield itself to a single yoke. She has, "with bare and bloody feet, climbed the steep road of wide empire," but to-day she stands at the top—mistress of the world. Man, with his talents, his strength, and his selfishness, has been tamed to her hand. The sensual, dominant brute with whom she began what Max Nordau calls "the toilsome, slow ascent of the long curve leading up to civilization," stands beside her to-day, hat in hand, her lover—husband; tender, faithful, courteous, and indulgent.

This is the conquest that has been made, the crown and throne achieved by the silent, uneducated woman of the past.

Monogamous marriage is the foundation stone on which has been built her power; a power which, while it has endured to her own benefit, has not been exercised for selfish ends. She has raised the relation between man and herself from a mere contract of sensuality or convenience to a spiritual sacrament within whose limits the purest and most exalted of human emotions find play. For the coarse indulgence and bitter enmities of polygamy has been substituted the happiest of bonds, in which the higher natures find room for the subtlest and completest felicities, and within which the man, the woman, and the child form a holy trinity of mutual love and well-being.

To this jewel, so hardly won, so long toiled for, it would be natural to suppose that woman would cling with all the force of her nature; all the more as education broadened her capacity for reflection and deepened her consciousness of self. On the contrary, the little learning she has so far acquired seems, as usual, a dangerous thing, and with the development of self-consciousness the keen, unerring *flair* of her instinct for the one thing needful has been blunted and enfeebled. It is not necessary to give undue weight to the blatant and empty-headed crew who announce marriage to be a failure, and that women are tired of, and will no longer submit to, child-bearing. There are crowing hens in all barnyards, and their loud antics never materially affect the price of eggs.

But that the women of our own time should treat marriage—that hard-won, dear-bought triumph—with such profligate recklessness amazes me. We are making ducks and drakes of the treasure heaped up for us by our mothers. How long will this imperfectly monogamous animal respect an institution which is all for our benefit, if we ourselves regard it so lightly?

The modern woman is so spoiled, so indulged, that she does not realize how much a man gives and how little he gets in marriage. He gives a half, sometimes—indeed often—more than half, of his earnings, his name and its honour, his protection and defence of her person, and a lifelong responsibility for her and her children, and he gets—what? Her person, and it is to be hoped her affection. The woman of the present day lays too much stress upon this gift of her person. She appears to think that this gift alone renders man her eternal debtor. To speak a little brutally, he knows that he can easily buy a like gift elsewhere and for a less price.

I remember that last year Alice complained of some of Ned's small foibles.

"Oh, you must be patient with him," I said. "Think how much he gives you; home, name, support, protection—everything. He works hard for you every day. You are under tremendous obligations to him."

"Well, if you put it that way—" she answered resentfully, "but don't I give him love and affection in return?"

"Yes," I countered triumphantly, "but he gives you equal love and all these other things beside. It seems to me there's no question who gives most."

She opened her eyes rather wide and looked thoughtful.

JULY 17.
The Ideal Husband.

It being the "silly season" a controversy is raging in the daily papers as to the ideal wife and the ideal husband, and much correspondence is occurring under various anonyms.

Alas!—the only ideal husband who ever lived married the only ideal wife ever born. They were cut off in the flower of their youth—some time during the first years of the Pliocene Period—and minute fossil fragments of their bones are now worn as relics by pious celibates, and are said to have worked miracles.

Of so potent an essence are their mere memories, it is said his knightly ghost haunts the rosy chambers of all maiden dreams, and men seeking Her like find all other women less desirable because of her fabled virtues.

I suppose all girls see him more or less in their lovers. Imagination deceptively moulds their features to a similacrum of that noble legendary person, until the fierce light which beats upon the married reveals the unprepossessing traits of plain everyday humanity. Yet every woman begins her sentimental life with hopes unabated by the depressing failures of others.

A most quaint and charming creature—this ideal who haunts the dreams of maidenhood! Compounded all of purity and passion, of chivalry and grace, of vigour and beauty. He can in moments of excitement tie the poker into love-knots, and has a hand of velvet with which to touch the dreamer's curls. A ruler of men, he is to be led by a single golden hair. Capable of volcanic passion, which renders him indifferent to meals or to fatigue, he can yet be moved to these ecstasies by but a single member of the sex, and despite snubs or coquetry can live for decades upon the mere hope of her favour. He excels in all manly prowess and diversions, and yet is never guilty of causing the loved one to mourn his absence during a golf widowhood. He adores poetry and is superior to all vulgar commercialism, and yet manages—in that simple fashion known only to ideals—to accumulate a fortune and be generous in the matter of diamonds. He combines in one stalwart person all the virtues of Galahad, Arthur, Launcelot, and Baron Rothschild.

Later on the wife develops an ideal less magnificently ornamental than this choice collection of bric-à-brac virtues. The married idol must be thoroughly domesticated: prepared to throw himself with enthusiasm into the study of croup and measles; is deeply versed in the matter of female domestic service, and yet so full of tact as to be able to obliterate himself at moments of domestic crisis. Like the ideal servant, he must be never in the way and never out of it. He must be uncritical of failure, yet capable of enthusiasm for success; unselfish as a saint, yet commanding the secret of worldly achievement; and above all he must be hopelessly blind to the virtues and charms of every woman but his wife.

Taste as to details may differ according to temperament, nationality, and social condition, but, broadly speaking, this delightful person with his eccentric combination of qualities figures in the abstract affections of all women.

But these are dreams; diversions of those pleasant moments when the human moth allows itself, with futile richness of imagination, to consider the star as a possible companion, and it seems useless to hope that such a person will ever appear in this sinful and unworthy world.

Perhaps from time to time a man who faintly reflects the luminous charms of this knightly husband-saint does arise to cheer and comfort the weaker sex and keep their hopes and ideals alive, but the "Mauds," and "Charlottes," and "Mrs. S. F. J.s," who have been extolling his attractions in print, seem not to have prayerfully considered whether they themselves were fit mates for, or capable of satisfying the ideals of, this wholly impossible he. There is far less talk about the ideal wife—for two reasons, I suppose. One is that men have less time for chattering generalizations, and the other—alas!—is that men are far less interested in women than are women in men.

The American is supposed to more nearly approach this high standard than the men of any other nationality, but that typical American husband of novels has, I must confess, always seemed to me a paltry, bourgeois creature, with the soul of a bank clerk, a neglected mind, and with a low estimate and a sort of amused indulgence of women as pretty, fantastic, inconsequent children with an insane greed of luxury.

Of course, it is heresy to say so, but my observation leads me to think that American women hold a general position far inferior to the women of Europe. The American man is pre-eminently generous to them in material things. Often while he slaves and goes shabby himself he is willing to metaphorically back a van up to the coal-hole and fill the cellar full of jewels, but he denies to his women that whose price is above rubies—his own society. Why is American society made up of women? What is the cause of our superfluity of women's clubs, committees, and classes? What place has the middle-aged or elderly woman in America except as the mother of her daughters, or the dispenser of her husband's hospitalities and charities?

After the period of sex-attraction has passed women have no power in America. Who ever sees here, as is so often seen in Europe, an elderly woman's drawing-rooms filled with politicians, financiers, artists, who come for the refreshment and stimulation of her ideas and conversation? Mentally American women do not interest American men.

JULY 23.
A New Law of Health.

Louisa has become a raging Christian Scientist.

A distant memory returns to me. Once upon a time there was a little girl who, after the manner of her sex, feared greatly all and sundry of certain fierce beasts, among which were to be enumerated rats, mice, bumblebees, and more vividly and especially *DOGS*—whose culminating direfulness was only to be expressed in italicized capitals. On a day, being bidden to go across the village street to deliver a note to an opposite neighbour, she set out, radiating the pleasing results of soap, brushes, and a clean pinafore, but on reaching the gate came to a sudden pause. A specimen of the worst of enemies, who seemed to the perspective of an eye only three feet from the ground to easily rival an elephant in size, lay prone across the path, lolling an intimidating tongue, and rolling an eye which, though outwardly calm, might be guessed to conceal a horrid intent. There was a swish of short starched skirts, a twinkle of bare knees, and appeal was made to that infallible power and knowledge which Providence has so wisely placed in mothers. Being a person of nimble imagination this particular parent, realizing that a mastiff as large in proportion to her own inches as this one was to the normal height of five years might well daunt her own courage, forbore to remonstrate or use reason.

"Here," she said placidly, "is a lump of sugar. Put it on your tongue and hold it there. Of course, no dog will touch a person who has sugar on her tongue."

And so fortified, Five Years set forth with a conviction of immunity that carried her triumphantly past the source of terror. The incident is not in itself, perhaps, of historic importance, but is a particularly vivid example of the absolute divorce in the undeveloped mind between the laws of cause and effect, and in no department of human thought has that divorce continued so long as in the science of health. Every one of us can revive out of childhood a memory of the balm that overspread the injured temple when a sympathetic nurse bestowed the richly deserved spanking upon the offending chair corner that had caused the pain, or applied the clearly indicated plaster of a kiss; and medicine in its long career has followed the intelligent example of the nursery. But while medicine as a science has passed out of this stage with the general growth of knowledge, the bulk of mankind still continues to put sugar on the tongue as a protection against dogs, to castigate chair corners, and to apply remedies as unknown to the pharmacopœia as the feminine kiss. Perhaps the stolen potato carried in the pocket, or the bit of red flannel bound on the left wrist, are not so trusted a remedy for the pangs of rheumatism as they were fifty years ago, and the dried heart of a mouse worn in a bag about the neck seems to have lost its potency against epileptic seizures, yet the very large sums spent annually upon patent medicines—rivalling in amount what is known in temperance circles as the "Drink Bill"—and the rise and popularity of innumerable mushroom "cures" and systems, proves that the laws of health are still as heterogeneous from the intelligence of the majority of mankind as are the laws of the differential calculus.

It would be diverting, were it not so pathetic, to see the constant endeavour on the part of the multitude to lift itself by its own hygienic boot-straps in the form of barefoot cures, mind cures, prayer cures, cures by clairvoyance, by magnetism, red or blue lights, or by pilgrimages and relics. The child moving about in worlds unrealized is still the father and epitome of the man, and sees no reason why his own will, or that of some Power wishing him individually well, should not break through the immutable sequence of cause and effect, or upset the machinery of the universe in his behalf. His childish "Let's pretend" sweeps away for the moment the dull persistency of facts and opens a world where it is possible to eat one's cake and have it too, and after dancing escape the bill for the fiddling.

Speaking accurately there is, of course, no such thing as a new law of health —such laws being of their very nature eternal—but a consciousness of the hygienic code is as new as was the discovery not more than a century ago of the forces of electricity, which had, though the most powerful agent upon the earth, lain ready to our hands unrecognized throughout recorded time.

The unfortunate fact that the world of knowledge is not a globe is shown by this—that if, in setting out toward a fixed goal of truth, one's face is turned in the wrong direction, no length of travel, no miracle of persistency, ever conducts to the haven where one would be. A truth of moral geography by no means universally accepted as yet, and indeed certain inherent tendencies of human nature, will forever prevent its unanimous acceptance, a chronic childishness of mind being so common that one would almost despair of the acceptance of any new truth, were it not that the adult intelligence of the few eventually imposes its conclusions upon the multitude, or enforces at least an outward concurrence. The immature-minded many are always lusting after a sign of the wonderful, and kicking against the pricks of plain truth. Bullied out of crediting the existence of ghosts and fairies, they earnestly engage in burning witches, and shamed out of such mistaken zeal fling themselves into the arms of spiritualist mediums, flirt with the theosophists, or die under the ministrations of Christian Scientists. The whole history of supernaturalism has been the history of travel in the wrong direction—a wrong turning that had its beginning in a childish impatience that would attain to its end by sudden leaps in lieu of dusty plodding along the highway that led by slow windings to the desired end.

Man found painful barriers of time, space, and physical decay fencing him out of his Eden of gratified desire, and like a child he straightway fell to dreaming of flying carpets, of magic lamps, of transmutable metals, of fountains of youth and elixirs of life. At first these miracles were thought to be the gifts of shadowy, higher powers, who were happily superior to the cruel limits of material existence, and might give their assistance according to their capricious elfin fancy. Later, man began to believe that in himself lay the powers which were to break the chains that bound him the unhappy slave of distance, of the need for labour, of the tyrannies of nature, with her resistless heat and cold, storm and flood, pain and age. A glimmering of the truth, this, at last, but only a faint reflection on the horizon of the rising sun, on which he had turned his back. There followed a period of fasts and macerations whose courage and persistency was to make the gods tremble in respectful terror—a triumph over material passions which should give an occult power over material limitations. The Buddhists stood moveless and speechless until the birds reared their young in their hair, and thereby were supposed to grow so mighty that the mountains rocked beneath the weight of their thoughts, and space and time were annihilated.

Superb energies, passionate patience and ardour, master intellects, were wasted in the long endeavour to find some means by which nature could be conquered and man made master of circumstance—all given fruitlessly; thrown into that bottomless pit of error never to be filled. And these earnest, misguided travellers—so blinded were they—when one of their number turned about in the other direction promptly fell upon him and beat him into submission, as one who would check the struggle towards light and knowledge. Even now that the fact is accepted that nature is to be conquered by her own natural means only, and that supernaturalism is a waste and quaking morass upon which no edifice of truth is to be reared, there are many —sadly many—descendants of Lot's wife casting longing glances back to the Sodom of their intellectual sins. It is nothing to them that having once faced about in the right direction the same amount of effort, properly directed, has achieved that for which the supernaturalists had for ages striven in vain.

Eating his due amount of food and attaching no mystical significance to anything, man tore his way through the heart of mountains, flashed his thoughts under the wastes of ocean, sent his voice across a thousand miles, sailed into the teeth of the wind, devoured space with steam, reared palaces more lofty than Aladdin dreamed of, and—his own Kobold—dived into the darkness and fetched up gold and gems more than the fairy tales ever knew. He made himself lord of the visible earth, of time, of distance, of wave and wind. He laid his hands upon all the forces which had awed his childhood and forced them to work miracles beside which the fables of the Kabbalists seemed tame and feeble. And in spite of this there remain men and women who are more awed by a banjo flying through a dark room than by the telephone; who find the untying of knots in a cabinet, or the clutches of damp hands when the lights are turned down, more important than the automobile. It is the attitude of mind of a child, who is more interested by rabbits coming out of a conjurer's hat than by wireless telegraphy.

There is as great an inequality in the inheritance of health as in the heirship of wealth or brains. Some are born with a fortune of vigour and soundness so large that not a lifetime of eager squandering will leave them poor, and others enter the world paupers of so dire a need that no charity of medicine will ever raise them to comfort; but most of us have just that mediocre legacy of vitality which makes us indistinguishable units in the mass. It lies in the hands of each to improve or waste that property as he chooses, for there are self-made men physically as well as financially, and spendthrifts of health come to as sorrowful an end as prodigals of gold. The body is a realm where a wise ruler brings happiness as surely as a foolish one ensures distress, and wisdom here, as elsewhere, lies in the observance of natural laws.

It is just these natural laws—simple, severe, inexorable—against which the majority chafe, for which some magic pill or potion is offered as a substitute. Temperance, cleanliness, activity, are the three cardinal virtues of the body, as faith, hope, and charity are of the soul. As tithes of mint, anise, and cumin are easier to render than the observance of law, justice, and judgment, so burnt-offerings of drugs are offered to the Goddess Hygeia in place of obedience to her regimen. After the excesses of the carnival came the brief rigours of the Lenten retreat, and after the Fat Tuesday of gluttony comes the short atonement of the "Cure" at some mineral spring, where the priests of health are yielded a complete but passing submission. It is easier to repeat incessant formulæ of prayer than persistently to keep one's self unspotted from the world, and it is easier for fat old sinners to paddle about barefoot in the dew at a Kneippe cure than to abandon at once and forever their little darling sins of greediness or indolence. One hears a constant cry of "Lo, Here!" and "Lo, There!" and all the world rushes to sit hopefully under blue glass or swathe itself in pure wool in the ever-renewed belief that some substitute may be found for the fatiguing necessity of obedience to the three rules.

Even yet ill health is considered as a sort of supernatural visitation rather than a certain result of the infringement of plain laws. I remember reading once a clever book, less popular than it deserved to be, which told of a country in the heart of the Andes in which the intelligent inhabitants looked upon crime as the unfortunate result of congenital temperament; a disease demanding sympathy and treatment; but ill health aroused only condemnation as a wilful infringement of wise and well understood laws. A bronchial case caused arrest and imprisonment, and friends of the family considered it rude to cough in the presence of the criminal's unfortunate family; but a severe attack of embezzlement was cause of polite condolence, and cards were left upon the invalid with kind inquiries as to whether he was receiving the best moral attention. An idea less whimsical than it may seem.

Paracelsus—who was accused of magic because his cures were effected by such simple means—always asserted that if he were allowed to absolutely direct a child's diet from its birth he could build up a constitution which might without difficulty be made to last out a century in undiminished vigour; and there are those who are prepared to accept literally the age of the antediluvian patriarchs, on the ground that as at that time bread had not been discovered, digestions never called upon to struggle with starch found no difficulty in sustaining life to Methuselah's term.

It is certain that the subtle but supremely important chemistry of nutrition has been shamefully neglected in favour of matters far less germane to happiness, and that the same skill which has developed the science of bacteriology and pursued the most elusive microbe to his most secret lair might have been more profitably applied. After the microbe has been found and named his dangerousness remains unattenuated. How much more valuable would be a knowledge—equally attainable—of exactly the amount and nature of the food for the best results of growth and health.

There is a farmer ant in the West Indies, who, in a carefully prepared soil, compounded of flowers and leaves, grows a tiny fungus on which he feeds. The eggs of this ant seem, when hatched, to produce creatures all alike, but through different feeding they develop into warriors, farmers, or queens, as may be needed. If through an accident the supply of warriors is dangerously lowered, larvæ being fed with the meat which nourishes farmers are transferred to the soldiers' nursery, and change of diet produces change of nature.

Ah! could we too know upon what meat to feed our Cæsars, or Roosevelts, that they might grow so great. What a much more important achievement that would be than the naming of microbes which would be impotent to injure a perfectly nourished body.

To know the law, to practise it daily—there is the secret of the fountain of youth, the elixir of life. These Christian Scientists, who practise the latest abracadabra to conjure away the effects of fixed causes, who dream that pain arises from sin, and can be abolished by faith, childishly overlook the fact that pain in itself is no evil, but rather a good. It is simply a telegraphic message sent over the nerve-wires to the brain to inform it that some member of the physical commonwealth is in danger and requires help.

Not by magic is health to be obtained. Flying carpets will not reach it. Fasts and prayers will not call it down from heaven. Fixed, immortal, the laws continue. Always unchanged; always inexorable. The wages of the sin of disobedience are disease.

July 24.
"Dead, Dead, Dead."

I wonder if there is still anyone in all the world to whom this date is important? And after all why should it be? In twenty-three years a whole generation has come into life; has wept and laughed, and loved and married, and produced another generation to do the same thing—and who remembers the roses that withered even yesterday?

───────────────

       Oh, wild, loud wind,
Who, moaning, as in pain,
Beats with wet fingers at my door in vain,
Dost thou come from the graves with that sad cry
Which pleads for entrance, and denied, goes by
To faint in tears amidst the freezing rain?

In here the live red fire glows again.
Of life and living we are full and fain.
Here is no thought of death, or men that die—
       Oh, wild, loud wind!

Why shouldst thou come then to my window pane
To wring thy hands and weep, and sore complain
That they alone all sad and cold must lie
In wet, dark graves, and we breathe not a sigh?
We have forgot. The quick and dead are twain,
       Oh, wild, loud wind!

───────────────

SEPTEMBER 6.
Verbal Magic.

J——— was reading me parts of his new book in manuscript to-day, and I objected that it lacked style. "Why, all the successful writers tell me that style is unnecessary," he said in an injured tone. "D——— says he just writes ahead and pays no attention to it. He says that the laboriousness of Stevenson and Flaubert has 'gone out' and the public are bored by it. And just see how successful D——— is!"

What was one to say? I merely tried to look convinced and begged him to continue. And yet Emerson said that when the distraught Hamlet cried to the mailed spirit of his father,

> "What may this mean,
> That thou, dead corse, again in complete steel
> Revisit'st thus the glimpses of the moon?"

he was so possessed by the verbal magic of the phrase that he could attend no more to the rest of the play.

Perhaps it is some penetrating assonance in that "complete steel"—in those sibilant repetitions of "revisit'st thus the glimpses"—that makes its witchery. Poe carefully analyzed the science of it—which is no science at all, but the inscrutable magic of inspiration. Such lines as

> "Came up through the lair of the lion
> With love in her luminous eyes"

are built upon that theory of liquid consonants and open vowels, and it has no magic at all, while "To Annie"—which was written without conscious plan— is full of it.

"Her grand family funerals" is instinct with that prickling delight of the magic of words, as is "the wizard rout" of the bodiless airs that blew through her "casement open to the night."

Tennyson's famous alliteration,

> "The moaning of doves in immemorial elms
> And the murmur of innumerable bees"

lacks glamour. One scents the intention.

> "Ay! Ay! oh ay!
> The wind that blows the brier"

recaptures the elusive charm, because of its wild, unconscious lyrism.

Fancy these absurd, ignorant young writers talking of style having "gone out"! Apparently they suppose it means "fine writing," in which nothing is more lacking than style. The essence of style, I suppose, is in the inspired, instinctive choice of words which present suddenly to the mind a *picture* of what the writer is talking about. The whole *clou* of Hamlet's phrase is that "glimpses of the moon." It makes one see the vague, intangible momentariness of the apparition. Sir Thomas Browne's famous "drums and tramplings of three conquests" gives just that flashing picture of the banners and rolling sounds of those long vanished invasions. And Keats's

> "Casements opening on the foam
> Of perilous seas in fairy lands forlorn"

presents the indescribable to the eye.

There is, of course, that other element of musical quality, and Hamlet's phrase is delicious for its strange, broken sibilations, but without the *picture* the alliterations and vowel sounds are but dead things. All the fine, rolling, organ-like sonority of Swinburne's Hymn to Proserpine would be tedious without the impressions of light and colour that palpitate through the lines. For style I can think of no better modern example than the concluding paragraph in Lafcadio Hearn's paper on the dragon-fly in the volume called Kotto:

"... then let me hope that the state to which I am destined will not be worse than that of a cicade or of a dragon-fly;—climbing the cryptomerias to clash my tiny cymbals in the sun,—or haunting, *with soundless flicker of amethyst and gold*, some holy silence of lotus pools."

October 8.
Hamlet.

Old Mr. A—— was most interesting to-night at dinner on the subject of the various Hamlets he has seen—apparently every actor of any importance who has attempted the part in the last sixty years; not only the English-speaking ones, but German and French as well. After dwelling upon all manner of details of the varied dress, business, scenery, and so forth, of the different men who have attempted the role, I asked him which of them all he considered to have been the best, and he decided after some hesitation that not one of them satisfied him completely. "Not one of them all," he concluded, "seemed to me to have a clear, comprehensive grasp of the essentials of the part. Each appeared to try to express some one phase of it, but you felt the thing as a whole escaped them." Which is, perhaps, not to be wondered at, since, so far, it appears, as a complete conception, to have escaped every one. No one of the Shakespearian scholars has expressed what definite meaning the play in its entirety conveyed to his mind.

Mr. A——'s talk interested me immensely, much more than any of those long-winded mystical triumphs of verbiage the Germans perpetrate. I have seen but two eminent actors in the part. Booth's Hamlet was, of course, only a noble piece of elocution, not an interpretation, and without vitality. Mounet Sully—but then all Frenchmen believe Hamlet mad, despite his express warning to Horatio—

> "How strange or odd so'er I bearmyself,
> As I, perchance, hereafter *shall think meet*
> *To put an antic disposition on …*"

And of his confidence to Guildenstern that he is but

> "Mad nor'-nor'-west. When the wind is southerly
> I know a hawk from a hernshaw."

Of course, I've a theory of my own about Hamlet. It seems to me that the difficulty most persons experience in endeavouring to penetrate what they call "the mystery" of the Prince's character arises from the fact that they read the play either carelessly or with some prepossession, to fit which they bend all that he says or does. The German critics blunder through forgetting how essentially sane and unmystical was Shakespeare in every fibre of his mind. To him the cloudy symbolism of the second part of Faust would have sounded very like nonsense. His interest was in man—the normal, typical man and his passions of hate, love, ambition, revenge, envy, humour….

To me the key to Hamlet seems to be a proper regard for the attitude of the mind of the seventeenth century toward the belief in ghosts. The Englishman of Shakespeare's day hardly doubted their existence, but was unsettled as to the nature and origin of spectres. Whether they were truly shades of the departed ones which they resembled, or were merely horrid delusions of the mind, projected upon it by some malign and hellish influence, they were not clear.

Hamlet says:

> "The spirit that I have seen
> May be the devil: and the devil hath power
> To assume a pleasing shape; yea, and perhaps,
> Out of my weakness and melancholy,
> (as he is very potent with such spirits)
> Abuses me to damn me: I'll have grounds
> More relative than this…."

Personally, my method of endeavouring to clear vexed questions is to make an effort to conceive of my own emotions and actions in a like difficulty. To understand Hamlet I try to imagine what my frame of mind would be if P—— had died, suddenly and tragically, during my absence. Hastening home in all the turmoil of grief and shock I find H—— has grasped all P——'s fortune and has promptly married M——, whom I had expected to find as afflicted as I. Naturally I would be deeply horrified and offended and greatly puzzled over such a situation. When one injects the warmth and power of one's own emotions into a situation by personifying it with one's own kinspeople one begins to realize Hamlet's condition of mind prior to the appearance of the Ghost. A ghostly visitation not being imaginable nowadays, one may suppose one's self having a vivid and circumstantial dream, making all these curious conditions clear by an explanation of hideous criminality. The hysterical distraction of Hamlet's interview with the Ghost seems natural enough when one pictures one's own horror and incredulity on awaking from such a vision.

Of course, a reaction would follow the first red lust for denunciation and for revenge of the deep damnation of the taking off of the helpless victim. One would be continually paralyzed in the very act of vengeance by the remembrance that one had no better authority than a dream for proof of crime in those one had always loved and trusted. The thing would seem so incredible, and yet the dream would explain all the puzzling facts so clearly. To a young and noble mind, evil in those one loves appears impossible. One would be always fighting the thought—which pulled the very ground of confidence from under one's feet—and yet always laying traps to prove one's

76

suspicions true, as the jealous notoriously do; wishing yet fearing to know the truth. Hamlet's varying fits of violence and indecision seem natural enough under the circumstances, and not a sign of madness nor of eccentricity of character. He is called the "Melancholy Dane," but to a young confiding heart the first revelation of the possibility of filth and criminality in those near in blood and love causes distrust of all the world; arouses a mad desire for escape out of a cruel existence where such spiritual squalour is possible. If one will bring the situation home to one's self in this way—vivifying it with one's own heart—Hamlet no longer seems a strange and alien soul, but one's very own self caught in a web of horrid circumstance, and doing and being just what one's self would do and be in like case. Temptation to suicide, murder, "unpacking one's heart with words," bitterness to, and distrust of, the innocent Ophelia, treachery, doubt, indecision,—all are inevitable temptations. Looked at in this way, there is no mystery at all in the play if one reads it straight and simply, and from the human point of view—which view was always Shakespeare's, I think.

DECEMBER 13.
Ghosts.

The R——s are home this week from California, and full of a surprising tale of their experience in renting and trying to live in a haunted house. They had no idea of its unpleasant character when they took it. Indeed they decided upon it principally because of the sunniness of the rooms and its generally cheerful character. The only suspicious feature was the very moderate price; but that appears to have aroused only gratitude instead of suspicion in their minds.

The sounds they heard, which finally drove them out of the house, were such commonplace ones—the clinking of medicine bottles, the mixing of stuff in saucers—that one hardly believes they could have invented them. Invention would certainly have conceived a more dramatic excuse for abandoning a house. Also, they solemnly aver that it was only upon their giving up the lease that they heard the story of the almost incredible tragedy of the former owner's death.

There certainly must be some manifestations such as are commonly known as "ghostly." I never have come across any personally, but the testimony is too frequent and persistent for doubt. Some phenomena have undoubtedly been observed of which the laws are not yet understood. The psychologists profess to be working in this direction, but the psychology of our day is still in about the condition of astronomy and chemistry in the days of the thirteenth-century astrologers and alchemists—mere blind flounderings. We need a psychological Copernicus badly. I am convinced that what are commonly called "superstitions" are really observed results of unknown causes. When I was a child the negroes always warned one that it brought bad luck to go near a stable when one had a cut finger. Nothing could seem more blindly uncorrelated, and yet it is now known that the germ of tetanus breeds only in manure, which shows that their observation was correct, though they had no conception of germs, or microbes. It was an old superstition, derided by the medical profession, that there was some merit in hanging red curtains at the windows of a smallpox patient; yet recently some interesting discoveries have been made as to the effect of red light upon sufferers from this disease.

Again there is the old-wife's belief that the howling of a dog presages death. I saw no sense in that until I was brought in contact with death for the first time, and then discovered that a person near the end, and immediately afterwards, emitted a powerful odour, very like the smell of tuberoses. In two cases within my experience this odour remained in the death-chamber, despite persistent airing and cleaning, for fully a year. My sense of smell is extremely acute, and no one seemed to remark this odour but myself, nor have I ever heard or seen any mention of the phenomenon being noticed by others; but naturally a dog, whose sense of smell must be a thousand times more acute than mine, is aware of this strange, half repulsive perfume, which has the effect upon his nerves produced also, apparently, by moonlight and by music.

If fresh rose leaves are shut closely into a drawer until they have thoroughly dried and crumbled, they will be found, when removed, entirely scentless, but the drawer will retain for years some intangible emanation which they have given off, and this will permeate any object left in the drawer. Recent delicate experiments have shown how the violence of emotion will affect the weight of human beings, and no doubt, in supreme crises of feeling, living bodies may lose this weight by the throwing off of some emanation which may linger for a long time in the immediate surroundings. It has been discovered that many objects retain luminosity, after being long exposed to powerful rays; a luminosity invisible to our sight, but sufficient to make dim photographs upon highly sensitized plates. The "ghosts" are very probably explicable on some such theory as this. Some individuals are like these extremely sensitive plates. The emanations thrown out in the condition of intense emotion affect them, and give them an impression of sounds or sights which appear, in our present state of ignorance, to be supernatural. Of course, any psychologist or scientist would pooh-pooh this hypothesis of mine, if it were made public, but equally they would have sniffed fifty years ago at a guess at wireless telegraphy, or the Roëntgen ray, or the radioactivity of radium. After all, however, they are right in thinking that guesses are not very valuable unless one has the industry to demonstrate their accuracy.

December 20.
Amateur Saints.

If there is any one thing more particularly repulsive to me than another it is the way the average clerical person speaks of religious things. One would suppose that such matters, if one really believed them, would be the profoundest sentiments of one's nature, and be mentioned with the reserve and reverence with which the lay person treats the deeper sentiments, such as love, honour, or patriotism.

A little pamphlet came by mail to-day, which proved to be a sort of begging letter from a community of Protestant clergymen, who are undertaking to imitate monasticism in America. Under a heading of a cross is this text, "If we have sown unto you spiritual things, is it a great matter if we shall reap your worldly things?" And there follows an appeal for assistance in building a monastery on the Hudson. The language of this pamphlet is the usual language of begging letters, only with that flavour of smug religiosity and bland business-like dealing with matters of the soul which amazes the lay mind.

This community of, presumably, able-bodied men who desire to reap of our worldly things naively sets forth in the following programme the manner in which they intend to occupy their time:

5 A.M.	Rise.
5.30 to 6.	Meditation in Chapel.
6.	Morning Prayer and Prime.
6.50 to 8.	Celebrations of the Holy Eucharist.
8.	Breakfast.
9.30.	Terce and Intercessions.
12 M.	Sext and None.
12.30 P.M.	Dinner.
1 to 1.20.	Recreation (in common).
4.45.	Evensong.
5.15 to 5.45.	Meditation.
6.	Supper.
6.30 to 7.15.	Recreation (in common).
8.30.	Compline.
10.	Lights extinguished.

And it is to permit them to spend their days in such fruitful fashion that one is called upon to contribute the money earned by men who toil! That many have already contributed is to be inferred from the fact that this community has become possessed of seventy-five acres of valuable land, and has spent some forty thousand dollars on the erection of a monastery.

Of course, there are worthless idlers everywhere, but very few of them in our practical day assume their indolence as a merit, or call upon their neighbours to support them, in the name of the deeper sentiments of life.

Hare, in "A Pair of Spectacles" remarks cynically, when asked to help an indigent widow, "Oh, I know that indigent widow; she comes from Sheffield." One knows these sturdy beggars. They come from out the Middle Ages, when it was still felt that there was some special virtue in abandoning the obvious duties of life to take up others more appealing to the Saint; more appealing precisely because they were anything but obvious.

The very name of Saint is a stench in my heretical nostrils. I never knew or read of one who was not a vain egoist, with all the cruelty, obstinacy, and selfishness of the egoist. Read the Lives of the Saints. Not one of these absurd chronicles but is a repulsive tale of an insane vanity trampling on the rights and feelings of others to achieve notoriety. St. Louis is a sample of the type: renouncing his duties to his unlucky wife, squabbling with every other monarch unfortunate enough to be associated with him, and wrecking the expeditions in which he joined because of some petty qualm about his meagre, unimportant little soul.

The person who extorts my reverence is not Saint Elizabeth, but that poor boy, her husband, bearing the torments of her hysterical squeamishness with such noble patience and chivalry. One can picture that tired, sleepy young fellow, busy with his duties of government all day, dragged out of his proper slumber to behold his ridiculous wife climbing out of bed to lie on the cold floor in her nightgown, while the attendants stood about and crossed themselves in admiration.

St. Theresa seems to have been a sort of Moyen-Age Hedda Gabler; no better than an ecclesiastic flirt. Go through the whole list and the story is always the same. One never hears of a person with a sense of humour—which implies a sense of proportion—setting up as a saint. The breath in the nostrils of these gentry is the stare of the unthinking multitude, who are awed by anything out of the ordinary. And yet it takes so much finer patience, so much greater self-abnegation, to do the plain duties of life. I feel far more like crossing myself when I look at the humble commuter, who has sat on a stool all day, and travels with his arms full of parcels to that cheap, draughty cottage in the cold dusk of Lonelyville, to listen patiently to Emily's recitals of Johnny's cut finger and Mary Ann's impudence. It is upon such as he that civilization and the world's happiness and sunshine depend. He has done a man's duties; upon him depends a helpless woman, and innocent children. His tedious, petty drudgeries rise to nobility compared with the lives of these fat and lazy grubs with their complines and sexts and primes.

St. Theresa seems vulgar to me contrasted with the anxious Emily cheapening chops at the butcher's, and fighting around the bargain counter to make her laborious commuter's meagre salary stretch over the needs of her family. It requires a finer and sweeter, a more saintly nature to walk the floor patiently with a teething baby than to pose as a saint on the floor to no one's benefit but one's own.

Ah, those humble, lovely souls bearing the whips and scorns of Time, and the spurns that patient merit of the unworthy takes—their commonplace daily halos make the saints' diadems look like imitation jewels.

JANUARY 1, 1900.
The Zeitgeist.

Back from the gates of the City of Life there runs a great highway, whose beginning is in the land—east of the sun and west of the moon—where the unborn dwell. It is a broad and well-trodden road; beaten smooth by the feet of the hurrying generations that tread sharp upon one another's heels as they press forward out of grey and airless nothingness into the warm atmosphere of existence.

By the side of this road lies a chimæra, with woman's breasts couched upon lion's paws. It is the old direful Questioner of Thebes; the Propounder of Riddles; the prodigious Asker of Enigmas. Before entering the gates of the City the jostling multitude must pause in their furious haste towards life and listen to her as she propounds to each generation her problem. Every generation guesses at the riddle with fear or hope, with timidity or courage, as its nature may be, and then rushes on within the gates, not knowing if it has guessed aright, but with the task laid upon it of living out its life by the light of that answer, let the result be what it will.

The Sphinx lies watching the generations whirled past her into existence. She listens to the cries, the turmoil, the bitter plaints of those within the walls who believed that they had solved her problem a century ago, and as she listens she smiles her cold, incredulous smile. Not yet have they divined her secret, if one may judge from their loud protests, and this new generation pouring in among them has but small patience with their failure. The newcomers are quite sure that they at last have answered the immortal conundrum correctly. They have found it quite easy, and they mean to show their silly predecessors how simple it is to find happiness if one has only the correct formula.

All the preceding guesses have been wrong?—well, but it is just because they were wrong that the application failed. Here is the right one at last, triumphantly evolved by the new heir of all the ages, and it will be soon seen how criminally, how almost incredibly mistaken the previous generations have been in their foolish attempts to live by such palpably absurd theories of existence.

Make way!—you silly old folk—make way for the young lords of life who come bearing truth and wisdom to the world! Who come to inaugurate a reign of peace and plenty and delight!

The old generation, nearing the City's lower gate,—beyond which lies another road, equally broad and well-travelled, but gloomier and more airless than the one by which they came,—shake their heads doubtingly at these assertions. They were quite as confident in their time, and yet, somehow, things did not work out as they expected. No doubt their own guess was quite right; they are almost sure of it; but many unforeseen exigencies interfered. People were obstinate. The formula was perfect, but people were so very wrong-headed that it never had a proper opportunity of proving how infallible it really was. And so difficulties in the application arose, and—But the young newcomers push them, still babbling and explaining, out of the further gate, and set at once about regenerating the unfortunate city which has been forced to wait such a weary while for this the perfect solution of all problems.

And the old Questioner lying without the gates stares with her long, calm eyes into the white mist from which yet more generations are to come, and she smiles her fixed and scornful smile.

It was after this fashion our century, nineteenth of the era, came in—flushed, happy, confident. It came an army with banners, every standard blazoned in letters of gold with its magic device—"Liberty, Equality, Fraternity."

How it hustled the poor painted, formal, withered, old eighteenth century out at the nether gate! Smashing its idols, toppling over its altars, tearing down its tarnished hangings of royalty from the walls, and bundling its poor antiquated furniture of authority out of windows. All doors were flung wide; the barriers of caste, class, sex, religion, race, were burst open and light poured in. The gloomy Ghettos were emptied of their silent, stubborn, cringing population; forged by the hammer of Christian hate through two thousand years into a race as keen, compact, and flexible as steel. The slave stood up free of bonds; half exultant, half frightened at the liberty that brought with it responsibilities heavier and more inexorable than the old shackles. Woman caught her breath and lifted up her arms. The old superstitious Asiatic curse fixed upon her by the church was laughed scornfully into nothingness. She was as free as the Roman woman again. Free to be proud of her sex, free to wed where she chose, free to claim as her own the child for whom she had travailed to give life.

A vast bonfire was made of the stake, the wheel, the gyve; of crowns, of orders, of robes of state. All wrongs were to be righted, all oppressions redressed; all inequalities levelled, all cruelties forbidden. Men shuddered when they thought of the crimes of the past, when they talked of Calas. Such a crime would never be possible in this new golden age. Only of oppression and cruelty was vice bred. Given perfect liberty and perfect justice the warring world would become Arcadia once more. Lions if not hunted, and if judiciously trained by the constant instilling of virtuous maxims, would acquire a perfect disgust for mutton, and lambs would consequently lie down beside them and would grow as courageous and self-reliant as wolves.

What a beautiful time it was, those first thrilling days of the new era! How the spirit dilates in contemplating it, even now. The heart beat with the noble new emotions, the cheek flushed, the eyes glistened with sensibility's ready tear. It was so pleasant to be good, to be kind, to be just; to feel that even the bonds of nationality were cast aside, and that all mankind were brothers striving only for pre-eminence in virtue. It was a new chivalry, a new crusade. Only, instead of lovely princesses to be succoured, or sepulchres to be saved, it was the rescue of all the humble and suffering, a crusade against the paganism of the strong. The heart could hardly hold without delicious pain this broad flood of universal kindness.

It was then that Anarcharsis Clootz presented to the National Assembly his famous "deputation of mankind."…

"On the 19th evening of June, 1790, the sun's slant rays lighted a spectacle such as our foolish little planet has not often to show. Anarcharsis Clootz entering the august *Salle de Manège* with the human species at his heels. Swedes, Spaniards, Polacks, Turks, Chaldeans, Greeks, dwellers in Mesopotamia come to claim place in the grand Federation, having an undoubted interest in it…. In the meantime we invite them to the honours of the sitting, *honneur de la séance*. A long-flowing Turk, for rejoinder, bows with Eastern solemnity, and utters articulate sounds; but owing to his imperfect knowledge of the French dialect, his words are like spilt water; the thought he had in him remains conjectural to this day…. To such things does the august National Assembly ever and anon cheerfully listen, suspending its regenerative labours."

It was at this time the big words beginning with capitals made their appearance and were taken very seriously. One talked of the Good, the True, the Beautiful, and the Ideal, and felt one's bosom splendidly inflated by these capitalized mouthfuls. There were other nice phrases much affected at the time—the Parliament of Man, the Federation of the World, *la Republique de Genre Humain*. The new generation was intoxicated with its new theory of life, with its own admirable sentiments.

Discrepancies existed, no doubt. The fine theories were not always put into complete practice. While the glittering phrases of the Declaration of Independence were declaring all men free and equal, some million of slaves were helping to develop the new country with their enforced labour. The original owners of the soil were being mercilessly hunted like vermin, and the women of America had scarcely more legal claim to their property, their children, or to their own persons than had the negro slaves. Nor did the framers of the Declaration show any undue haste in setting about abolishing these anomalies.

The National Assembly of France decreed liberty, equality, and fraternity to all men, and hurried to cut off the heads and confiscate the property of all those equal brothers who took the liberty of differing with them.

But it was a poor nature that would boggle at a few inconsistencies, would quench this fresh enthusiasm with criticism. After all, mere facts were unimportant. Given the proper emotion, the lofty sentiment of liberty and good-will, the rest would come right of itself.

A new heaven and new earth, so it seemed, was to be created by this virile young generation who had rid themselves of the useless lumber of the past. The period was one of universal emotion, exhibiting itself in every form: in iconoclastic rages against wrong—rages that could only be exhausted by the destruction of all the customs, laws, and religions that had bound the western world for two thousand years; it showed itself in sanguinary furies against oppression—furies which could be satiated only by seas of blood; in floods of sympathy for the weak that ofttimes swept away both strong and weak in one general ruin. It was displayed in convulsions of philanthropy so violent that a man might not refuse the offered brotherhood and kindness save at the price of his life. The cold dictates of the head were ignored. The heart was the only guide. Is it any wonder that driven by the wind of feeling and with the rudder thrown overboard the ship pursued an erratic and contradictory course. Seen in this way one is no longer surprised at the lack of consistency of the *Declaration des Droits de l'Homme*, that declared "All men are born and continue free and equal in rights"—that "Society is an association of men to preserve the rights of man"—that "freedom of speech is one of the most precious rights," and yet that France, crying aloud these fine phrases, slaughtered even the most silent and humble who were supposed to maintain secret thoughts opposed to the opinions of the majority. It is no longer astonishing to read the generous sentiments of our own Declaration and to remember the persecutions, confiscations, and burnings that drove thirty thousand of those not in sympathy with the Revolution over the borders of the New England States into Canada, and hunted a multitude from the South into Spanish Louisiana. One is no longer amazed to hear de Tocqueville declare that in no place had he found so little independence of thought as in this country during the early years of the Republic. By liberty—his adored liberty —the revolutionary sentimentalist meant only liberty to think as he himself did, and the whole history of man records that there is nothing crueller than a tender heart ungoverned by a cooler head. It is in this same spirit that the inquisitor, yearning in noble anguish over souls, burns the recalcitrant. It is plain to him that such as are so gross and vicious as to refuse to fall in with his admirable intentions for their eternal welfare can be worthy of nothing gentler than fire.

But whatever the discrepancies might be, the whole state of feeling was vastly more wholesome, more promising, than the dry formalism, the frivolous cynicism which it had annihilated and out of which it had been bred. The delicate, fastidious, selfish formalists of the eighteenth century were naturally aghast at the generation to which they had given birth. It was as if an elderly dainty cat had been delivered of a blundering, slobbering, mastiff puppy, a beast which was to tear its disgusted and terrified parent in pieces. No doubt they asked themselves in horror, "When did we generate this wild animal that sheds ridiculous tears even while drinking our blood?" Not seeing it was the natural child and natural reaction from the selfish short-sightedness of *"Que ne mangent ils de la brioche?"* from the frigid sneer of *"Apres nous le deluge."*

This torrent of emotionalism to which the nineteenth century gave itself up is amazing to our colder time. It manifested itself not only in its public policy, in its schemes for universal regeneration, but it completely saturated all the thought of the time, was visible in its whole attitude toward life. Madame Necker could not bear the thought of her friend Moulton's departure after a short visit, so that he was obliged to leave secretly without a farewell. She fainted when she learned the truth and says, "I gave myself up to all the bitterness of grief. The most gloomy ideas presented themselves to my desolate heart, and torrents of tears could not diminish the weight that seemed to suffocate me"—and all this about the departure of an amiable old gentleman from Paris to Geneva!

They had no reserves. The most secret sentiments of the heart were openly discussed. Tears were always flowing. Nothing was too sacred for verbal expression. They wrote out their prayers, formal compositions of chaste sentiments, and handed them about among their friends as Italian gentlemen did sonnets in the Quattro Cento. On anniversaries or special occasion they penned long epistles full of elegant phrases and invocations to friends living under the same roof, who received these letters next morning with the breakfast tray, and shed delicious tears over them into their chocolate.

"A delicate female" was a creature so finely constituted that the slightest shock caused hysterics or a swoon, and it was useless to hope for her recovery until the person guilty of the blow to her sensitiveness had shed the salt moisture of repentance upon her cold and lifeless hand and had wildly adjured her to *"live"*—after which her friends of the same sex, themselves tremulous and much shaken by the mere sight of such sensibility, "recovered her with an exhibition of lavender-water" or with some of those cordials which they all carried in their capacious pockets for just such exigencies. Nor did the delicate female monopolize all the delicacy and emotionalism. The Man of Feeling was her fitting mate, and the manly tear was as fluent and frequent as the drop in Beauty's eye. Swooning was not so much in his line; there was less competition, perhaps, for the privilege of supporting his languishing frame, but a mortal paleness was no stranger to his sensitive countenance, his features contracted in agony over the smallest annoyance, and he had an ominous fashion of rushing madly from the presence of the fair one in a way that left all his female relatives panting with apprehension, though long experience might have taught them that nothing serious ever came of it.

Thus the Nineteenth Century entered upon its experiment with the verities, beginning gloriously; palpitating with generous emotion; ready with its "blazing ubiquities" to light the way to the millennium. The truth had been discovered, and needed but to be thoroughly applied to ensure perfect happiness. By 1840 the tide of democracy and liberalism had risen to flood. The minority were overawed and dumb. To suggest doubts of the impeccable ideals of democracy was to awaken only contempt; as if one should dispute the theory of gravity. It was *chose jugée*. It did not admit of question. The experiment was in full practice and the new theory, having swept away all opposition, had free play for the creation of Arcadias.

Alas! Thus in the eighteenth period of our era had Authority cleared the ground. It had burned, hanged, shut up in the Bastille all cavillers, and just as the scheme had a chance to work it crumbled suddenly to pieces in the blood and smoke of revolutions. Democracy had no fear of tragedy from the very nature of its principles, but it had decreed liberty, and liberty began to be taken to doubt its conclusions. There began to arise voices bewailing the flesh-pots and the lentils of the ruined House of Bondage. Democracy had brought much good: that was not denied, but alas, what of the old dear things it had swept away, the sweet loyalties, the ties between server and served. The enormous social and political edifice reared by feudalism had had black dungeons, noisome cloacæ, no doubt, but what of its rich carvings, of its dim, tender lights filtered through flowered traceries? Where was its romance, its pageants and revels? The rectangular, ugly, wholesome building, which democracy had substituted as a dwelling for the soul of man, with its crude, broad light flooding every corner, failed to satisfy many who forgot all the bitter inconvenience of the ancient castle, remembering in homesick longing only its ruined beauties and hoary charm.

Science in its hard unsentimental fashion commenced to demonstrate the fallacy of the heart's ardent reasoning. She stripped the lovely veil from nature's face, and showed the tender springing grass of the fields, the flushed orchard blossoms, the nesting bird, the painted insect floating in the breeze,— all, all engaged in a ferocious battle for life—trampling on the weak, snatching the best food, always either devouring or devoured. It had been decreed with thunderous finality that the feeble should be by law placed on equality with the strong, and this was announced as the evident intention of beneficent nature. Science, however, relentlessly demonstrated that nature was not beneficent; that in fact she was a heartless snob, and that to "Nature's darling, the Strong," she ruthlessly sacrificed multitudes of the helpless. Democracy had made itself the champion of the humble, had cursed the greedy and powerful; science proved that the humble and unaggressive were doomed, as was proved by their not surviving in the terrible struggle for life that was raging in all forms of nature, and of which the human mêlée was but an articulate expression. The conviction that humanity had once known perfect equality, and that freedom had been filched by the unscrupulous, was shown to be quite unfounded. Rousseau's Contrat Social was made absurd by Darwin's Descent of Man. All research tended to prove that from the earliest Pliocene it was not the weak or the humble, but he who

> "Stole the steadiest canoe,
> Eat the quarry others slew,
> Died, and took the finest grave,"

who had founded families, developed races, brought order out of chaos, had made civilizations possible, had ordained peace and security, and had been the force of upward evolution.

It was thus that the freedom which the heart had given to the head was used to prove how fallible that generous heart was.

Then out of all of this groping regret, out of this new knowledge, there arose, with excursions and alarums, Carlyle; the first who dared frankly impeach the new theory and decry its results. Through all his vociferousness, through all his droning tautology, his buzzing, banging, and butting among phrases like an angry cock-chafer, through the general egregiousness of his intolerable style, there rang out clear once again the pæon of the strong. Here was no talk of the rights of man. His right as of old was to do his duty and walk in the fear of the Lord.

… "A king or leader in all bodies of men there must be," he says. "Be their work what it may, there is one man here who by character, faculty, and position is fittest of all to do it."

For the aggregate wisdom of the multitude, to which Democracy pinned its faith, he had only scorn.

... "To find a Parliament more and more the expression of the people, could, unless the people chanced to be wise, give no satisfaction.... But to find some sort of King made in the image of God, who could a little achieve for the people, if not their spoken wishes yet their dumb wants, and what they would at last find to be their instinctive will—which is a far different matter usually in this babbling world of ours" ... *that* was the thing to be desired. "He who is to be my ruler, whose will is higher than my will, was chosen for me by heaven. Neither, except in obedience to the heaven-chosen, is freedom so much as conceivable."

Here was the old doctrine of the divine right of the strong man to rule, come to life again, and masquerading in democratic garments.

No revolution resulted. Democracy did not fall in ruins even at the blast of his stertorous trumpet, but the serious-minded of his day were deeply stirred by his words, more especially as that comfortable middle-class prosperity and content, to which the democrat pointed as the best testimony to the virtue of his doctrines, was being attacked at the same time from another quarter. Not only did Carlyle scornfully declare that this bourgeois prosperity was a thing unimportant, almost contemptible, but the proletariat—a new factor in the argument—began to mutter and growl that he had not been given his proper share in it, and he found it as oppressive and unjust as we had found the arrogant prosperity of the nobles intolerable.

That old man vociferous has passed now to where beyond these voices there is peace, but the obscure mutterings of the man in the street, which was then but a vague undertone, has grown to an open menace. The Sphinx smiles as she hears once more the same cries, the same accusations. We of the middle classes, who threw off the yoke of the aristocracy, clamoured just such impeachments a century back. We are amazed now to hear them turned against ourselves. To us this seems an admirable world that we have made; orderly, peaceable, prosperous. We find no fault in it. It has not worked out, perhaps, on as generous lines as we had planned, but on the whole each man gets, we think, his deserts.

We ask ourselves wonderingly if the aristocrat of the eighteenth century did not, perhaps, see his world in the same way. He paid no taxes, but he thought he did his just share of work for the body politic; he fought, he legislated, he administered. Perhaps it seemed also a good world to him; well arranged. Perhaps he was as indignant at our protests as we are at those of to-day. We thought ourselves intolerably oppressed by his expenditures of the money we earned, by his monopoly of place and power; but we argue in our behalf, that as we pay the taxes we should decide upon the methods of the money's use and have all the consequent privileges. What, we ask ourselves angrily, do these mad creatures, who are very well treated, mean by their talk of slavery —of wage-slavery? How can there be right or reason in their contention that the labourer rather than the capitalist should have the profit of labour? Does not the capitalist govern, administer, defend?

Attacked, abused, execrated, we begin to sympathize with those dead nobles, who were perhaps as honest, as well-meaning, as we feel ourselves to be; who were as disgusted, as scornful, as little convinced by our arguments as we by those who accuse us in our turn of being greedy, idle feeders upon the sweat of others. Perhaps to him the established order of things seemed as just and eternal as it does to us. We begin to have more comprehension of that dead aristocrat.

For a hundred years now democracy has had a free hand for testing its faiths and ideals. Let us reckon up the results of this reign of liberty, equality, fraternity.

Out of the triumphant bourgeoisie has grown a class proud and dominant as the nobles of old days. They have wealth, luxury, and power, such as those nobles never dreamed of. Capital is organized into vast, incredibly potent aggregations. Labour in its turn has organized for itself a despotism far-reaching, unescapable, which the old régime would never at its haughtiest have ventured upon. The two are arrayed against one another in struggles of ever-increasing intensity.

The Brotherhood of Man is still a dream. The continent of Europe is dominated by two autocratic sovereigns, who overawe others by the consistent and continuous policy only possible to a despotism. The republics of France and of South America are the prey of a horde of adventurers who only alternate despotisms; the armaments of the world are so pretentious that each fears to wield so terrible a weapon. The great nations are dividing the weak among themselves as lions do their prey. All nations are exaggerating their barriers and differences. Russia is repudiating the Occidental languages and civilizations which she at first received so gladly. Hungary has abandoned the German tongue, and the Hungarians, Czechs, and Bohemians, held together by the bond of Austria, are restive and mutually repellent. The Celt revives and renews his hatred of the Saxon, and in Ireland and in Wales the aboriginal tongues and literatures are being disinterred and taught as a means of destroying the corporate nationalism of the British Isles. The Bretons disclaim their part and interest in France. The Spanish empire has fallen into jealous and unsympathetic fragments. The Hindus are clamouring for an India for the Indians. All are rivals; envenomed, and seeking domination. And America,—America, the supreme demonstration of the democratic ideal,— what of her? America has embarked upon imperial wars: refuses sanctuary to the poor and oppressed as inadmissible paupers, and laughs at the claims to brotherhood and citizenship of any man with a yellow skin.

The church, which is most opposed to individual liberty of thought, has been reconquering great territory in the very citadels of free conscience. One large body of Protestants is repudiating its protests against irresponsible authority, and basing its claims rather upon appeal to ancient precedent.

Science has one by one torn in pieces and scattered the iridescent bubbles of democracy's sentimental visions. The Ghetto is open, but the Jews are still persecuted. A Calas is no longer sacrificed to bigoted churchmen, but an intolerant army make possible the Affaire Dreyfus. Zola, after a century of democracy, is called upon once more to take up the work of Voltaire. Woman is still waiting for political equality with man. But perhaps the most surprising result is man's change in his attitude towards himself. *Man*, who spelled himself with reverent capital letters, who pictured the universe created solely for his needs,—who imagined a Deity flattered by his homage and wounded by his disrespect—Man, who had only to observe a respectable code of morals to be received into eternal happiness with all the august honours due a condescending monarch, had fallen to the humility of such admissions as these....

"What a monstrous spectre is this man, the disease of the agglutinated dust, lifting alternate feet or lying drugged with slumber; killing, feeding, growing, bringing forth small copies of himself; grown upon with hair like grass, fitted with eyes that glitter in his face; a thing to set children screaming;— ... Poor soul here for so little, cast among so many hardships filled with desires, so incommensurate and so inconsistent; savagely surrounded, savagely descended, irremediably condemned to prey upon his fellow lives, ... infinitely childish, often admirably valiant, often touchingly kind; sitting down to debate of right or wrong and the attributes of the Deity; rising up to battle for an egg or die for an idea.... To touch the heart of his mystery we find in him one thought, strange to the point of lunacy, the thought of duty, the thought of something owing to himself, to his neighbour, to his God; an ideal of decency to which he would rise if possible, a limit of shame, below which if it be possible he will not stoop.... Not in man alone, but we trace it in dogs and cats which we know fairly well, and doubtless some similar point of honour sways the elephant, the oyster and the louse, of whom we know so little"—

Alas, Poor Yorick! How a century of liberty has humbled him. It is thus the successors of Rousseau, of Chateaubriand, of the believers in the perfectibility of man, speak—saying, calmly, "The Empire of this world belongs to force"—and that "Hitherto in our judgments of men we have taken for our masters the oracles and poets, and like them we have received for certain truths the noble dreams of our imaginations and the imperious suggestions of our hearts. We have bound ourselves by the partiality of religious divinations, and we have shaped our doctrines by our instincts and our vexations.... Science at last approaches with exact and penetrating implements ... and in this employment of science, in this conception of things, there is a new art, a new morality, a new polity, a new religion, and it is in the present time our task to discover them."

We must not forget to consider a little the amusing change our century has seen in the alteration of its heroic ideals. For the sentimental rubbish, the dripping egotism of a Werther, of a Manfred, in whom the young of their day found the most adequate expression of their self-consciousness, we have substituted the Stevenson and Kipling hero—hard-headed, silent, practical, scornful of abstractions, contemptuous of emotions, who has but two dominant ideals, patriotism and duty; who keeps his pores open and his mouth shut.

The old democratic shibboleths still remain on our lips, are still used as if they were truisms, but in large measure we have ceased to live by them, we have lost all our cocksureness as to their infallibility. We give frightened sops to our anarchical Cerberus. We realize that despite all we so proudly decreed the strong still rule and plunder the weak, and weak still impotently rage and imagine a vain thing of legislation as a means of redressing this endless inequality.

Much of good we have given. How could an ideal so tender, so beautiful, so high of purpose, fail of righting a thousand wrongs?

How could those sweet, foolish tears fail to water the hard soil of life and cause a thousand lovely flowers of goodness and gentleness to bloom? That we have not solved the riddle of the Sphinx, that we have not found the secret of happiness, is hardly cause for wonder or shame. Neither will our successors find it, but it is interesting to speculate as to what clue they will use to guide them in the search. It is plain that our ideals, our formulæ, are being cast aside as inadequate, but the new century is coming in with no programme as yet announced. It is thoughtful, silent; it avoids our drums and shoutings and vociferous over-confidence.

What will be its Time-Spirit, since ours plainly will not serve? Will the wage-earners shear the bourgeoisie of their privileges as we shore the nobles a century ago—or will liberty sell herself to authority again in return for protection against the dry hopelessness of socialism, or the turmoil of anarchy? Or will the new generation evolve some new thought, undreamed of as yet—some new and happier guess at the great central truth at which we forever grasp and which forever melts and eludes?

FEBRUARY 11.
The Abdication of Man.

In the midst of all these excursions and alarums of war, and preparation for war, a sudden and great silence has fallen upon the everlasting discussion of the relations of the sexes. Before the stern realities of that final and bloody argument of Republics, as well as of Kings, further dissection of the Women Question has been deferred. The most vociferous of the "unquiet sex" have been regarding respectfully the sudden transformation of the plain, unromantic man who went patiently to business every morning in a cable car, and sat on a stool at a desk, or weighed tea, or measured ribbon, into a hero ready to face violent annihilations before which even her imagination recoils. The grim realisms of life and death have made the realism of such erstwhile burning dramas as The Doll House shrink into the triviality of a drama fit only for wooden puppets. Sudden and violent readjustments of ideas are apt to be brought about when human relations are jarred into their true place by the thunder of cannon. War legitimatizes man's claim to superiority. When the sword is drawn he is forced to again mount that ancient seat of rule from which he has only recently been evicted; or rather from which he has himself stepped down. The democracy of sex at once becomes ridiculous—the old feudal relation reasserts itself.

It is interesting to note that there has not been one feminine voice raised to protest against the situation. The entire sex, as represented in this country, has, as one woman, fallen simply and gladly into the old place of nurse, of binder of wounds, of soother and helpmeet. Not one has claimed the woman's equal right to face villainous saltpetre, or risk dismemberment by harbour mines.

I believe this to be because woman prefers this old relation. I believe that if man were willing she would always maintain it; that it depends upon him whether she returns to it permanently or not. I believe that her modern attitude is not of her own choosing—that man has thrust that attitude upon her. For the oldest of all empires is that of man; no royal house is so ancient as his. The Emperors of Japan are parvenus of the vulgarest modernity in comparison, and the claims of long descent of every sovereign in Europe shrivel into absurdity beside the magnificent antiquity of this potentate. Since the very beginning of things, when our hairy progenitor fought for mastery with the megatherium, and scratched pictorial epics upon his victim's bones, the House of Man has reigned and ruled, descending in an unbroken line from father to son in direct male descent. His legitimacy was always beyond dispute; his divine right to rule was not even questioned, and was buttressed against possible criticism not only by the universal concurrence of all religious and philosophic opinion, but by the joyful loyalty of the whole body of his female subjects. Moses and Zoroaster, St. Paul and Plato all bore witness to his supremacy, and the jury of women brought in a unanimous verdict in his favour without calling for testimony.

Women yet living can recall a day when they forgot their pain for joy that a man-child—heir to that famous line of kings—was born into the world. They can remember a time when their own greatest claim to consideration rested upon the fact that they were capable of perpetuating the royal race. They recollect a period when even from his cradle the boy was set apart to be served with that special reverence reserved for those whose brows are bound with the sacred circlet of sovereignty—when a particular divinity did hedge even the meanest male; a tenfold essence being shed about all those who were of the House of Aaron.

Why then—since all this is of so recent existence, since man's rule was founded so deep on woman's loyalty—has he been swelling the melancholy ranks of Kings in Exile? For that he has ceased to reign over woman does not require even to be asserted. It is self-evident.

When was this amazing revolution effected? Who led the *emeute* that thrust man from his throne? It is a revolt without a history; without the record of a single battle. Not even a barricade can be set up to its credit, and yet no more important revolution can be found in the pages of the oldest chronicles. So venerable, so deep-rooted in the eternal verities seemed the authority of man over woman that the female mind, until the present day, never doubted its inevitableness. Indeed, as is the case with all loyal natures, she was jealous for the absolutism of her master, and was quick to repair any such small omissions as he himself might have made in the completeness of his domination. All of her sex were trained from their earliest infancy to strive for but one end—to make themselves pleasing to their rulers. Success in the court of man was the end and aim of their existence, the only path for their ambition, and no other courtiers ever rivalled these in the subtle completeness of their flattery. Man's despotism, of course, like all other tyrannies, was tempered by his weaknesses, but while woman wheedled and flattered and secretly bent him to her projects she did not question his real right to govern.

Here and there through the past there arose a few scattered pioneers in recalcitrance. One of the first to deny the innate supremacy of the male was a woman who herself wore a crown. Elizabeth Tudor had a fashion of laying heavy hands upon her rightful lords whenever they displeased her, and she appears to have rejected the whole theory of feminine subordination. John

Knox—strong in the power of the priest, whose sublimated prerogatives man had skilfully retained in his own hands—could and did dominate Mary Stuart even upon the throne, but when he blew from Geneva his "First Blast of the Trumpet Against the Monstrous Regiment of Woman," and called all the ages to witness that the rule of a female was an affront to nature that trenchant lady who held the English sceptre forbade him ever again to set foot in her domains, and before he could do so, in his need, he had to digest a most unwholesome dose of humble pie.

Elizabeth, however, was a unique personality and had few imitators. The literature of her day abounds with expressions of supreme humility and loyalty from the one sex to the other. Elizabethan poets deigned to play at captivity and subjection to the overwhelming charms of Saccharissa and her sisters, and turned pretty phrases about her cruelty, but this was merely poetic license of expression. All serious, unaffected expression of conviction, such as was to be found in the religious writings of the time, and in the voluminous private correspondence, which gives us the most accurate description obtainable of the real actions and opinions of our ancestors, never suggested a doubt of man's natural and inalienable superiority, mental, moral, and physical. So undisturbed was this conviction, down almost to our own day, that the heresy of Mary Wollstonecraft gave the severest of shocks to her own generation. So heinous seemed her offence of *lèse-majesté* in questioning man's divine right that one of the most famous of her contemporaries did not hesitate to stigmatize her as "a hyena in petticoats."

History gives us but one record of a general outbreak. In the thirteenth century the Crusades had so drained Europe of its able-bodied men that the women were forced to apply themselves to the abandoned trades and neglected professions. They shortly became so intoxicated by the sense of their own competency and power that when the weary wearers of the cross returned from the East they were at first delighted to discover that their affairs were prospering almost as well as ever, and then amazed and disgusted to find the women reluctant to yield up to their natural rulers these usurped privileges. Stern measures were necessary to oust them. Severe laws were enacted against the admission of women into the Guilds—the labour organizations which at that period governed all the avenues of industrial advancement; and the doors of the professions were peremptorily slammed in the women's faces. Such episodes as these, however, were detached and accidental. Female treason never dared unrebuked to lift its horrid head until within the present generation.

The emancipated new woman has various methods of accounting for the humbling of this hoary sovereignty. Some find it only a natural concomitant of the general wreck of thrones and monarchical privilege—in other words, that it is but one phase of advancing democracy. By some it is supposed that in this Age of Interrogation man's supremacy, along with all other institutions, has been called upon to produce an adequate reason for being, and producing no answer that seems satisfactory, he has been summarily forced to abandon pretensions which rested merely upon use and wont. It is said by some that woman has been examining with coldly unprejudiced eye the claim of man to rule, has been measuring his powers against her own and has not been daunted by the comparison. The more noisy declare that she has stripped him of his royal robe and that, like Louis XIV., minus his high heels and towering peruke, she finds him only of medium stature after all; that she has turned the rays of a cynical democracy upon the mystery encompassing his Kingship and refuses to be awed by what she sees there; that it is because of this she begins to usurp his privileges, thrust herself into his professions, shoulder him even from the altar, and brazenly seating herself on the throne beside him she lifts the circlet from his brows to try if it be not a fit for her own head.

The weakness of all such explanations is that they do not take into account the fact that woman is not by nature democratic. Whatever political principles the occasional or exceptional woman may profess, the average woman is in all her predilections intensely aristocratic;—is by nature loyal, idealistic, an idolater and a hero worshipper. Strong as the spirit of democracy may be, it could not by itself alone in one generation change the nature of woman. The explanation must lie elsewhere.

In the language of a now famous arraignment—"*J'accuse*" man himself.

No ruler is ever really dethroned by his subjects. No hand but his own ever takes the crown from his head. No agency but his can wash the chrism from his brow. It is his own abdication that drives him from power—abdication of his duties, his obligations, his opportunities. Ceasing to rule, he ceases to reign. When he ceases to lead he wants for followers, and the revolt which casts him from power is only the outward manifestation of his previous abdication of the inward and spiritual grace of kingship. When man ceased to govern, woman was not long in throwing off the sham of subjection that remained.

Like other subjects, woman required of her master two things—*panem et circenses,*—bread and circuses. When the industrial changes brought about by the introduction of machinery put an end to the old patriarchal system of home manufactures, man found it less easy to provide for his woman-kind— more especially his collateral woman-kind—and without any very manifest reluctance he turned her out into the world to shift for herself. Here was a shock to her faith and loyalty! The all-powerful male admitted his inability to provide for these sisters, cousins, aunts, and more distant kin who had looked up to him as the fount of existence, and had toiled and fed contentedly under his roof, yielding to him obedience as the natural provider and master. Woman went away sorrowful and—very thoughtful.

This alone was not enough to quite alienate her faith, however. Woman was still, as always, a creature of imagination—dazzled by colour, by pomp, by fanfaronade. She was still a creature of romance, adoring the picturesque, yielding her heart to courage, to power, to daring and endurance—all the sterner virtues which she herself lacked. The man of the past was often brutal to her—overbearing always, cruel at times, but he fascinated her by his masterfulness and his splendour. She might go fine, but he would still be the finer bird. When she thought of him she was hypnotized by a memory of gold, a waving of purple, a glitter of steel, a flutter of scarlet. He knew that this admiration of hers for beauty and colour was as old as the world. From primordial periods the male has recognized this need of the female. The fish in the sea, the reptile in the dust, the bird in the forest, the wild beast in the jungle are all aware of their mates' passion for gleaming scales, for glowing plumes, for dappled hides and orgulous crests of hair. They know, they have always known, that no king can reign without splendour. Only man, bent solely upon his own comfort and, it would seem, upon the abandonment of his power, deliberately sets himself against this need of the female, which has become imbedded in her nature through every successive step up in the scale of evolution. He alone fatuously prides himself on the dark, bifurcated simplicity of his attire, intended only for warmth and ease and constructed with a calculated avoidance of adornment. To avoid criticism he has set up a theory that a superior sort of masculinity is demonstrated by the dark tint and unbeautiful shape of garments (as if the fighting man, the soldier—who is nothing if not masculine—were not always a colourful creature); and chooses to ignore or resent woman's weakness for this same gold-laced combatant, and for the silken, picturesque actor.

"*J'accuse*" the man of abandoning his mastership and becoming a bourgeois in appearance and manner through a slothful desire for ease. There can hardly be a question that Louis le Grand's red heels and majestic peruke were uncomfortable and a bore, but his sense of humour and his knowledge of men were such that his bed curtains were never untucked until his lion's mane had been passed in to him on the end of a walking stick, and was safely in its place. He could imagine how unimposing the King of Beasts might be in *négligé*. He knew that to be reverenced one must be imposing. Louis the Unfortunate found it far less tedious to abandon stateliness, and work wigless and leather-aproned at his locksmith's forge, while his feather-headed queen played at being a dairy-maid at Trianon, forgetting that the populace, which had submitted humbly to the bitter exactions of the man who dazzled them, seeing the bald head and leathern apron would get abruptly up from its knees and say: "What! submit to the pretensions of a locksmith and a dairy-maid—common folk like ourselves—certainly not!" and proceed to carry their sovereign's suggestion of equality to the distressingly logical conclusion to be found at the mouth of the guillotine.

"*J'accuse*" man of carrying further this democracy of sex by adding rigid plainness of behaviour to ugliness of appearance, forgetting that a woman, like the child and the savage, love pomp of manner as well as of garment, and that what she does not see she finds it hard to believe. Every wise lover soon learns it is necessary to reinforce the tenderness of his manner by definite assurances of affection several times in every twenty-four hours. Then, and then only, is a woman sure she is loved.

How can she believe man heroic unless he use the appearance and manner of the hero?

Sir Hilary of Agincourt, returning from France, found his lady from home, and he and all his weary men-at-arms sat there—mailed cap-à-pié—throughout the entire night until she returned to welcome them home and receive their homage. What if at other times Sir Hilary may have been something of a brute? Lady Hilary, flattered by this fine piece of steel-clad swagger, would, remembering it, forgive a thousand failures of temper or courtesy.

When El Ahmed held the pass all through the darkness while his women fled across the desert, and his foes feared to come to hand grips with him, not knowing he stood there dead,—propped against the spear he had thrust into his mortal wound to hold himself erect—there was no female revolt against the domination of men who were capable of deeds that so fired women's imaginations.

These may, after all, seem to be frivolous accusations—that men do not dress well; do not behave dramatically; but the signification of these seemingly capricious charges lies deeper than may appear. Man has been seized with a democratic ideal, and after applying it to political institutions has attempted to carry it into domestic application. He is relentlessly forcing a democracy of sex upon woman; industrially, mentally, and sentimentally. He refuses to gratify her imagination; he insists upon her development of that logical selfishness which underlies all democracy, and which is foreign to her nature. Now, nature has inexorably laid upon woman a certain share of the work that must be done in the world. In the course of ages humanity adjusted itself to its shared labours by developing the relation of master and defender, of dependent and loyal vassal. Sentiment had adorned it with a thousand graces and robbed the feudal relation of most of its hardships. Mutual responsibilities and mutual duties were cheerfully accepted.

Woman was obliged to perform certain duties, and these could only be made easy and agreeable by sentiment, by unselfishness. Man needed her ministrations as much as she needed his. He realized that sentiment was necessary to her happiness and he accepted the duty of preserving that sentiment of loyalty and admiration for himself which made her hard tasks seem easy when performed for a beloved master. He took upon himself that difficult task of being a hero to a person even more intimate than his valet. He took the trouble to please woman's imagination.

The hard democracy of to-day will take no note of the relation of master and dependent. Each individual has all the rights which do not come violently in contact with other's rights, and has no duties which are not regulated by the law. Unselfishness is not contemplated in its scheme. Every individual has a right to all the goods of life he can get.

Women are beginning to accept these stern theories; beginning to apply the cruel logic of individualism. So far from the power to win his favour being her one hope of advancement or success, she does not hesitate to say on occasion that to yield to his affections is likely to hamper her in the race for fame or achievement. So far from the giving of an heir to his greatness being the highest possibility of her existence, she sometimes complains that such duties are an unfair demand upon her energies, which she wishes to devote exclusively to her own ends.

The universal unpopularity of domestic service proves that the duties of a woman are in themselves neither agreeable nor interesting. Where is the man in all the world who would exchange even the most laborious of his occupations for his wife's daily existence? The only considerations that can permanently reconcile human beings to unattractive labours is first the sentiment of loyalty—that such labours are performed for one who is loved and admired—and second the fine, noble old habit of submission. These incentives to duty, these helps to happiness, man has taken from woman by weakly shuffling off his mastership.

I accuse man of having wilfully cast from him the noblest crown in the world —of having wrongfully abdicated. War has at least this merit that it forces him to drop the vulgar careless ease of the bourgeois and resume for the time at least those bold and vigorous virtues which made him woman's hero and her cheerfully accepted master.

JUNE 13.
Life.

It is a toy: a jingling bauble gay,
That children grasp with wondering, wide-eyed pleasure;
Soil it with too fierce use, and find their treasure
But rags and tinsel, which at close of day
Falls from their weary hands. It is a page
Whereon the child scribbles unmeaning scrawls.
Youth's glowing pen indites sweet madrigals.
Man tells a history, and sad old age—
Seeing that all the space that he hath writ before
But wrote in varying ways his folly large—
Sets "Vanity" upon the meagre marge.
And last Time prints "The End" and turns it o'er.

JULY 2.
Portable Property.

The Chinese pinks are in full bloom now. I have gathered pounds of them and arranged them in vases, and the mere outline of their feathery grey-green foliage, set with those fringed flecks of warm colour, makes existence seem an agreeable thing. The sound of children's voices outside, the smell of the cut grass, and the blue of the day, all seemed freshly sweet and pleasant because of the pleasure the freaked beauty of the bowls full of pinks give me. I am sorry for the people who don't care for flowers. The amiability they always awake in me is one of my most valued bits of secret property. That is the kind of possession that moth and rust cannot corrupt. It is safe from burglars, and even age does not wither one's satisfaction in such belongings. Most of my life I have been poor, as the world reckons poverty, but in reality I have owned more than many millionaires.

It seems to me a wise thing to store up private wealth early. My nose to me a kingdom is, and emperors and any millionaire might envy me the possession of my ears and eyes. There are pale-souled philosophers who declare their contempt for the power of gold, and some narrow dull-witted folk are really oppressed by luxury—all of which seems nonsense to me; but if one can't and most of us can't, have high stepping horses, good frocks, paid service, and expensive homes, one can at least own tangible treasures of smells and sights and sounds. And, ah! the odd bits of poetry I possess....

> Now rising through the rosy wine of thought
>   Bright-beaded memories sparkle at the brim
> Of the mind's chalice. Golden phrases wrought
>   By the great poets bubble to its brim.
>
> My poets—as the patterned skies are mine,
>   The perfumes and the murmurs of the sea
> Are all mine own—their cadences divine
>   Seem as my goodly heritage to me.
>
> They trace the measures of all hidden things,
>   And into worded magic can translate
> The hidden harmonies which Nature sings;
>   Her mighty music inarticulate.
>
> And who will list hears sonorous vibrations
>   As though their thoughts strung harps from earth to heaven

That rung with golden, glad reverberations
As wide-winged dreams breathed through their strings at even.

July 10.
Are American Parents Selfish?

P—— overwhelmed us last night at dinner by declaring that American parents were selfish. We dropped our fish-forks and stared at him in amazement and disgust. H—— said, severely, "You are a foreigner." P—— couldn't truthfully deny it, and the bare statement seemed sufficient, but H —— likes to clinch any nail he drives and he went on:

"It is admitted by every unprejudiced person—excepting, of course, the ignorant and benighted foreigner—that the Americans are the people, and that wisdom and virtue will necessarily die with them; that all their customs and institutions, whether social or political, are the wonder, the envy, and despair of other nations, which makes an assertion like yours seem almost frivolous."

"Selfish!" I struck in, "selfish—indeed! on the contrary, the American is blamed as the most indulgent of parents. Surely selfishness is the last charge that can justly be made."

P—— tried to defend himself. He admitted that "if indulgence invariably implied unselfishness the American would certainly have nothing with which to reproach himself in his relations with his children."

We fought the question over until late, and this is about what our discussion came to. There can be no doubt that a fond gentleness of rule is in this country, the law of the average household. So far as is compatible with common sense, the children have entire liberty of action, and, so far as the means of the parents permit, the children are provided with every advantage and pleasure. Indeed, to such lengths at one time did fondness go that it too often degenerated into a laxness that made the American child a lesson and a warning to other nations. Daisy Miller and her little, odious toothless brother were supposed to typify the results of this fatuous feebleness of rule in our family life, but neither Daisy nor her brother can now be held to be typical pictures, though their prototypes still exist here and there. The American parent of to-day rules more firmly and with greater wisdom. Such figures as those of the unhappy girl and the odious boy brought home to us the truth—forgotten in our passion for universal liberty—that a relaxation of wise, strong government by the parent was cruelty of the most far-reaching and irreparable sort.

No doubt Henry James' mordant satire helped to inaugurate a salutary reform, and it is just possible that a new work of a similar nature is now needed to suggest further serious reflections to American parents; to rouse them to consider whether their whole duty is performed in seeing their children well fed, well educated, and raised to man's estate. With most parents the sense of responsibility ceases when the boy begins to earn his own living, when the girl dons orange blossoms. Like the birds, the American parent works hard to feed the nestlings, carefully teaches them to fly, and then tumbles them out into the world to fend for themselves. So far in our history this elemental method has worked well, no doubt. The result of it has been to breed the most precocious, self-reliant, vigorous, irreverent race the earth has yet seen. One may see the whole situation epitomized in the orchard any pleasant June day —an astonished fledgling ruffling his feathers upon some retired bough, ruminating upon the sudden shocks and changes of existence, and afraid almost to turn his head in the large, new, lonesome world surrounding him. As the hours pass his melancholy reflections are pierced by hunger's pangs. Heretofore, a busy parent has always appeared to assuage such poignant sensations, but now that hard-worked person may be seen—genially oblivious of obligations—refreshing himself with cherries, and the fledgling, with a squawk of wounded amazement, discovers for the first time that even parents are not to be depended upon. His hunger meantime grows. An opportune insect flits by and is snapped at involuntarily. It proves to be of refreshing and sustaining quality, and digestion brings courage. A hop and a flutter show the usefulness of wing and limb. More luck with insects demonstrates that the world belongs to the bold, and before the day is done the cocky young nestling of yesterday is shouldering his papa away from the ripest cherries.

All this is very well in a world where flies and cherries are free to all, but America is fast ceasing to be a happy uncrowded orchard in which the young find more than enough room and food for the taking.

In the past, the boy—inured to plain living and a certain amount of labour from childhood—had only to take the girl of his choice by the hand and go make a home out of virgin soil, wheresoever chance or fancy led, himself and his parents both confident he could not suffer in a land where only industry was needed to ensure conquest. These boundless possibilities relieved the parent of half the cares incident to the relation, and that sense of freedom from responsibility has remained, while conditions have altered. The bird-like fashion of refusing further liability once the child has made his first flight is still the rule.

To the European parent this seems a most flagrant abandonment of duty. There the anxious care for the offspring reaches out to the third and fourth generation, and every safeguard which law or custom can devise is thrown around the child. From the moment of its birth the parent of Continental

Europe begins to save, not only for the education and upbringing, but for the whole future existence of the child. It is not alone the daughter who is dowered, but the son also has provision made for his married life, when, as his parents keenly realize, the greatest strain will be made upon his resources and capabilities.

In America it is the custom—very nearly the universal custom—for the parents to spend upon the luxuries and pleasures of the family life the whole income. The children are educated according to this standard of expenditure, and are accustomed to all its privileges. No thought is taken of the time when they must set up households for themselves—almost invariably upon a very different scale from the one to which they have been used. To the American parent this seems only a natural downfall. He remarks cheerfully that he himself began in a small way, and it will do the young people no harm to acquire a similar experience—forgetting that in most cases the children have been educated to a much higher standard of ease than that of his own early life. The parents do not consider it obligatory to leave anything to their children at death. They have used all they could accumulate during their own lifetime; let their children do the same. The results of the system are crystallized in the American saying: "There are but three generations from shirt sleeves to shirt sleeves." The man who acquires wealth spends what he makes. His children, brought up in luxury, struggle unsuccessfully against conditions to which they are unused, and the grand-children begin in their shirt sleeves to toil for the wealth dissipated by the two preceding generations.

Europeans frequently and curiously remark upon the American's prodigality of ready money. The small change which they part with so reluctantly the American flings about with a fine mediæval profusion. The manner of life of the average well-to-do person in this country permits of it. The average man who earns ten or twenty thousand a year invests none of it. He installs his family in a rented house in the city in winter. Several servants are kept; the children are sent to expensive schools. All the family dress well, eat rich food, and indulge in costly amusements. In summer they either travel abroad, live in a hotel at a watering place, or rent again. The man's whole income is at his disposal to spend every year. None of it is deducted to be safely stored in property. When his daughters marry he expects their husbands to be solely responsible for their future, and if they do not succeed in marrying wealth, why so much the worse for them. When his sons begin their career he looks to them to be self-supporting almost from the first, and not to undertake the responsibilities of a family until they are able to bear such a burden without aid from him. He cannot assist them without materially altering his own scale of living, which he is naturally loath to do. At his death the income generally ceases in large part, and his widow, and such children as may still be unplaced in life, are obliged to relinquish the rented houses and the way of life to which they have been used.

To a Frenchman such an existence would seem as uncertain and disturbing as is generally supposed to be that of a person who has built upon the crust of a volcano. He could not contemplate with equanimity the thought of chaos overtaking the ordered existence of his family upon his demise. *Après nous le deluge* seems to him the insouciance of a maniac, or of a monster of selfishness. Daily expenditure is regulated within a limit which permits of a constant investment of a margin. When his daughter marries he insures in her carefully guarded dower that she shall continue her existence on somewhat the same scale to which she has been accustomed, and, in case of premature widowhood or accident of fortune, she and her children shall not be called upon to face the desperate strait of absolute pennilessness. He may deny her in her girlhood many of the indulgences common to her American prototype, but he denies himself at the same time in saving to insure the security and comfort of her future. The French father would think it terrible that a tenderly nurtured daughter should be suddenly thrust into abject dependence upon a husband who may possibly abuse the power given him by that circumstance, nor would he be more satisfied to think that she should, during her first years of married life, while still young and encountering the strain of motherhood, be called upon to face narrow means and a perilously uncertain financial condition.

When the son arrives at maturity the economies to which he, in company with his parents, has submitted, bear fruit in substantial aid in beginning his career, and he is not obliged to put out of his mind all thought of marriage during his youth, since his parents, and those of the woman of his choice, have provided for this very contingency through all the years of his minority.

The French—with the logical inevitableness of their mode of thought—carry this view of life to its extreme limit, but throughout all Europe, including England, the responsibility of the parent is more broadly conceived than in this country, where the excuse for an infinity of cheap flimsiness is the cynical phrase, "It will last my time." Men build cheaply, and forbear to undertake work of which they cannot see the immediate result, because there is no sense of obligation to the coming generation. The democratic theory is that each man must fight for his own hand; no debt is owed to either ancestry or posterity. The mind is not shocked by sudden destruction of families, by the sharp descent in the social scale, or the flinging of women into the arena of the struggle for life. The parent is quite willing to share with the child the goods of existence as far as he can achieve them, but he is unwilling to deny either child or himself that the child may benefit alone, or after he is gone.

Conditions in America are constantly assimilating themselves more and more to those existing in the older countries, where the conflict for existence is close and intense, and where the prudent, the careful, and the far-sighted inevitably crowd out the weaker and more careless individuals and families. An almost unmistakable sign of "an old family" in America is conservatism in expenditure and modes of life. The newly rich, who set the pace of public luxury, are always amazed at the probates of the wills of these quiet citizens. They cannot believe that one who spent so little should have so much, not realizing that the simplicity of life made it possible to solidly invest a surplus. The heirs of this solid wealth have been bred to prudence and self-denial. Such a family survives, while in all probability the offspring of the other type may in two generations be hopelessly trodden into the mire.

There is in the breasts of many parents a half-resentful feeling that they should not be asked to sacrifice themselves to the new generation. They insist upon their own right to all that is to be got out of life, feeling that what they give to the children is never repaid. This selfish type forgets that in doing their duty they are but returning to their children what they themselves received from the past generation, and that the children will in turn pay to their descendants the inherited debt of honour with interest.

July 30.
A Question of Heredity.

I was lunching out to-day, and sat beside Mrs. C—— S——. She told me her daughter was so hoping that the new child would be a girl. Four boys seemed a superfluity of masculinity in one household.

"I wish there was some way of knowing beforehand about such things," she complained.

"When F—— came," I said, airily, "there was the same feeling in our family; we all wanted so that she should be a girl. H—— was so comforting. He said she certainly would be, if there was anything in heredity; her mother was a girl, and all her aunts, and both her grandmothers. And she did turn out to be a girl, you see."

Mrs. C—— S—— looked at me with her mild blue eyes, and said, happily —"I wonder if there is really anything in that; for you know it's just the same in our family!"

OCTOBER 6.
The Little Dumb Brother.

I have been reading in one of the magazines a record of travel in the Rocky Mountains of the Arctic regions. It is illustrated with pictures of some ten polar bear skins—two of them evidently mere babies of bears—a dead ram, a dead caribou—the former killed, the author explains, to furnish the first food he had in forty-four hours. He concludes his article with this naive charge: "Wolves, when pressed by hunger, do not hesitate to fall upon one of their own number and sacrifice it to their beastly cravings. They are utterly lacking in conscience, and the young or weak of every class of land animals suffer from their wanton lack of mercy."

Such wicked wolves! And how about those baby bears?

It is the same point of view as that of the Spanish bull fighters. "They are not Christians—they have no souls—why consider them?"

As I have said before, very probably the decent, well-behaved, kindly Roman citizen of Nero's day, returning with his family from a pleasant afternoon at the gladiatorial shows, gathered his children about the household altar, offered pious libation to the gods, and went peacefully to bed with a clean and untroubled conscience. It was all simply a question of the point of view. A Roman citizen was certainly not going to be disturbed by a sense of wrong-doing in watching the pangs of such creatures as Christians or barbarians.

The theory that human beings were each and every one in a spiritual sense, brothers, came later to trouble this fine old crusted indifference, and now after nearly two thousand years the idea has so completely infiltrated human consciousness, that the death agonies of men can no longer anywhere serve as diversion to the gentle and the good. But behind that sweeping assumption that we of all organic nature alone possess that element of immortality, binding us together with spiritual ties, and laying upon all the mutual obligations of justice and mercy, we have been nourishing a towering and brutal egotism, that moves blindly and stupidly about amid unreckonable multitudes of sentient fellow creatures; unaware of their lives, their passions, or their languages. Contracted inside the shell of this foolish prepossession we miss half the interest and wonder of the world we inhabit, and—thinking of ourselves all the while as an honest and merciful fellow—we play an unimaginable devil to our unhappy neighbours.

And yet I think even we at our worst would recoil could there be set before us in plain language the immitigable horrors of man's place in nature written from the point of view of even the most philosophic and amiable of the beasts. It makes the skin upon one's flesh crisp to reflect how black would be that long chronicle of poisonings, burnings, slayings, devourings. Those unmentionable tortures upon the vivisector's table; those maimings and clippings of well-loved pets to gratify a cheerful but perverted fancy; the treachery, ingratitude, and fantastic despotism practised every day, and always —throughout the whole indictment set forth by the accusing animals,—would be seen a dark, everflowing stream of innocent blood, spilled purely for man's idle recreation. The fanged Nero of the jungle, the very Heliogabalus of the cobras would seem spotless saints contrasted with this horrid record of the deeds of what are commonly called kindly and upright men. The beasts had never need to invent a devil myth. The model was always to their hand.

Cardinal Newman once remarked, with a sense of surprise, that "we know less of the animals than we do of the angels," and when one remembers the disproportionate attention given the two subjects this is hardly cause for wonder. One of the favourite texts of the never-ending debates of the schoolmen of the Middle Ages was the question whether sixty thousand angels would have room to stand on the point of a needle; and upon this and cognate subjects

> … "Doctor and Saint—they heard great argument
> About it, and About: and ever more
> Came out by that same door wherein they went."

But of any study of what we call—in our topping human fashion—"the lower orders of creation" the history of the schools contains not a single record.

Even since science has begun to divert the world's mind from the study of the macrocosm, to the contemplation of the microcosm this same ingrained contempt and misunderstanding of the animals has led to the most amazing ideas. Descartes, whose study of the reflex actions of the muscles curiously anticipated some of the subtlest discoveries made recently in Chicago by Professor Loeb, propounded the theory, in his "Réponses," that animals were mere automata—which ate without pleasure, cried without pain, desired nothing, knew nothing, and only simulated intelligence as a bee simulates a mathematician. He says: "Among the movements that take place in us there are many which do not depend upon the mind at all, such as the beating of the heart, the digestion of food, nutrition, and respiration, walking, singing, and other similar actions when they are performed without the mind thinking of them. And when one, who falls from a height throws his hands forward to save his head, it is in virtue of no ratiocination that he performs this action. It does not depend upon his mind, but takes place merely because his senses being affected by present danger some change arises in his brain which affects the nerves in such a manner as is required to produce the motion, in the same manner as in a machine, and without the mind being able to hinder it. Now since we observe this in ourselves, why should we be so astonished if the light reflected from the body of a wolf into the eye of a sheep has the same force to excite it into the motion of flight?"

Why on the other hand should we refuse to think that the light reflected from the body of a lion into the eye of Descartes himself should have the power of exciting him into the motion of flight, without his mind being concerned in the matter at all—except that Descartes himself would assure us with his own lips that this was not so.

Our ignorance of the dialects of animals, our inability to understand the medium by which they convey their thoughts, makes it possible for men of even Descartes' abilities to generate such childish hypotheses. Even Huxley says blandly of animals that "Since they have no language they can have no trains of thought," though he admits that most of them possess that part of the brain which we have every reason to suppose to be the organ of consciousness in man.

It is one of the most regrettable results of this human egotism, which has dug so deep and permanent a gulf between ourselves and our fellow creatures, that we have made no concerted or intelligent effort to find a means of communication with our fellow beings. That such an effort would produce results worth the labour it would entail we have reason to infer from the surprising success that has followed our struggles to elucidate the meaning of the fragments of language sculptured on the broken stones that have been left by races extinct for thousands of years. We know how great are the barriers the varying tongues raise between living peoples: how much effort must be given to acquire a language foreign to us, even when surrounded by the sound of it in our daily life, and assisted by teachers, yet supreme human ingenuity has, from these fragments of broken stones, reconstructed dead tongues and forgotten histories of civilizations that for millenniums have been but dust blown through voiceless deserts. Yet in all the great lapse of ages during which man has been living in close intimacy with his domesticated animals not the slightest attempt has been made to cross the width of silence lying between him and his faithful companions.

The student who makes the acquaintance of animals only in the trap or upon the vivisection table may well assert that the beast has

"No language but a cry,"

but those who approach their fellow beings with a mind divested of this self-righteous cant are well aware that the animals have means of communication as accurate as our own, and fully sufficient for all the needs of their existence.

To an ant the man standing beside him is as a creature three thousand feet high, would be to us. Now let us imagine this colossal person stooping to examine the tiny beings hurrying to and fro in a channel between a row of structures built of fragments that would appear to him no bigger than grains of sand. He would, of course, be unaware that this channel was called Broadway, or the Strand, or the Avenue de l'Opera.

"Do these tiny atoms think, reason, or speak?" he would ask himself. His ear, of course, would be unable to catch any vibrations of their infinitesimal tones, but he would notice here and there two of them pausing to touch their forepaws, remaining opposite one another for some moments moving their minute lips, and that thereupon one or the other would abandon his travel along this channel and move off in another direction, apparently led thereto by the communication of a command or suggestion from his companion. If this giant should chance to be an intelligent giant he would certainly infer that these men had a language.

Now let us step out upon the grass any day in June and in our turn use an intelligent eye. Here lies a dead grasshopper. A foraging ant comes wandering by. He surveys it carefully and estimates the horse power requisite to move it, and then hurries away in the direction of home. Meeting another ant he stops, touches antennae for a few moments, and passes on. The second ant makes straight for the grasshopper and finds it without trouble. Nothing can be plainer than that the first ant told the second one where to go. "A glorious windfall!" he probably said, "There's a dead Leviathan about two miles from here. Keep straight on till you come to a three-cornered rock, then turn to the left and you will come upon three grains of sand and a straw. Climb the straw, and you can't miss it. It's big enough to be seen a mile away." The second ant, when it finds the grasshopper, does not go home. It sits down and waits till the first one returns with a great gang of labourers, and then every one seizes hold of a leg or wing and the stupendous mass is slowly removed to the nest. Would any person with ordinary common-sense suppose these to be automata?

Had Huxley pondered the Scriptures and gone to the ant to consider her ways he would have certainly been cured of his haughty illusions, for not only has each species of ant a language in which he can communicate with other ants of the same species, but each nest or clan has, clearly, its own brogue; for an ant knows instantly whether another belongs to its own nest or not. The ants of one nest murder those of another. It is a point of honour with them.

We have seen that Huxley admits reluctantly that most animals have those portions of brain development that we believe to be the seat of consciousness, but here is an insect with organs and functions as heterogeneous from our own as can well be imagined, and yet there is no mode of life that men have tried which one or another of the races of ants is not pursuing to-day. Beside the agriculturists and herdsmen, some keep slaves to do everything for them, some live by hunting and plunder, while others quarter themselves upon us and live by confounding meum and tuum. Any ardent pomologist may study the herdsmen tribes by simply turning over the leaves of his young apple tree in the spring. Upon the broad succulent meadows of the under side of his foliage he will discover fat flocks of aphis cows, tended by brawny ant cowherds, who keep a special eye upon the big brown bulls around which the cows and calves gather to feed. The herdsmen conduct them from leaf to leaf as they exhaust the sap, and at night by the long twig paths and barky roads they carry the milk of the sweet honey dew with which they are swollen. If the horticulturist be hard of heart and smear away a whole herd with a sweep of his thumb, the horrified herdsmen will rush frantically home, bursting into the nest to report to some hyksos king of the termites, that the Philistines have fallen upon his charge and that "I, only I, have escaped to tell the tale!"

The most interesting of the agricultural races of ants is that one commonly known in the West Indies as the parasol ant, from its fashion of carrying bits of flower petals over its shoulder at the angle commonly used with a sunshade. This ant erects an enormous structure, as large in proportion to its size as is the City of London to any one of its inhabitants. The dwellers in these cities are divided into classes: farmers, road-makers, explorers, nurses, soldiers, street sweepers, policemen, and, of course, the Queen. The great town is kept perfectly clean and sanitary by the scavengers, who remove all refuse every day. In case of death the bodies are removed some distance and buried. The soldiers guard the entrances to the city, and in case of attack by one of the Attila hordes of the barbarian hunter ants, they fight with a fury and courage so great that only after the entire army is destroyed is the city ever given up to pillage.

The explorers belonging to the nest scour the surrounding country in search of the material needed by the farmers, and following their indications, the road-makers clear paths a quarter of an inch in width and frequently a mile in length, through the immense tangles of the tropical forests,—roads as straight and useful as those of the Romans. Along these the farmers pass, often at the end of it to climb a tree fifty feet high in search of the bits of flower petals, with which they pass so continuously to the nest that the human observer will sometimes see what appears to be a thin trickle of pink or yellow through the jungle grass as far as the eye can reach. These flower petals are packed in the city's cellars, moistened, and sown with the spores of a minute fungus upon which the ants live.

Most curious of all is that these ants also keep pets—several varieties of tiny insects which they feed and protect, and which apparently serve no purpose save to give pleasure by their playful gambols. In every well established city of the parasol ants there resides a small green snake in a chamber built about him by the ants themselves, who feed and guard him, and when by any accident the little reptile is removed they abandon all their affairs until another is found to replace him. Unless this snake serves them as a fetish or deity there is no means of accounting for their desire for his presence, for as far as can be discovered he fills no purpose of utility. Mark Twain declares that the ants "vote, keep drilled armies, hold slaves and dispute about religion," and for all we know this little snake may be the centre of a complex system of theology.

Consider too Maeterlinck's "Life of the Bee," that remarkable study of a civilization so unlike our own. It is common to dismiss the bee's geometrical abilities with the futile word *instinct*, but honest students of the work of these astonishing insects have shown that, given a new situation to deal with, they first hold active counsel together concerning it, and then adapt their means to new conditions with all the skill and flexibility that suggest powers of trained reasoning. Here is a race that works for an ideal. The general good of the hive inspires in them as inflexible a severity, as ardent an abandonment of the desires of the individual as did the Roman patriotism of the elder Brutus, or of the young Scaevola. No more remarkable story is to be found in literature than Maeterlinck's description of the nuptial flight of the Queen Bee. Choosing a warm and perfect day in the very prime of the season's glow, distilling as she goes some intoxicating aroma—impalpable to our grosser senses—a perfume of love that drives every drone of the hives in passionate ardour to that deadly encounter, to which only he may obtain who can follow her arrowy course into the blue, where, out of sight of our feeble eyes, that one lethal embrace occurs after which the lover comes hurtling from the skies, dead and eviscerated. To provide this lover, whose potent tenderness shall ensure a myriad generation—this lover with greater wing flight than any of his fellows—with countless facetted eyes, with greater body and stronger limbs, this creature of such passion as to sacrifice his life for one moment of joy—the unflagging life work of not less than five of the sexless workers must be given, and hundreds of drones are raised each year that among them one may prove strong enough to attain to that dizzy aerial love.

Beside the stern, homogeneous, self-sacrificing civilization of the bees that of even the Japanese shows but clumsy, disordered and inadequate.

Many of the doings of these small brothers of ours seem incomprehensible and unreasonable to us, but imagine that three thousand foot giant looking down upon the mites in France and Germany in 1870 without an inkling as to the Spanish succession; upon the recent incredible scufflings and passagings back and forth over the veldts of South Africa without being instructed as to the term of residence required to obtain the franchise. To his ignorant eye how purposeless, how amazingly futile the whole affair would have seemed. And it is thus we move, stupid and contemptuous, amid great races and events, heavily indifferent to their meaning, to their significance to ourselves. We walk surrounded by powers whose forces we ignore, who work out their ends independent of us, yet against whom we are sometimes forced to battle mightily for existence. To the unreflecting man in the street the cinch bug seems a matter of small interest. No one interviews the coddling moth to inquire his intentions. War correspondents pass by the locust and ignore the cotton worm; the fly weevil and the ox bot seem to such an one but a feeble folk, yet every year in the United States alone these small races cost us more than three hundred and fifty millions of dollars, destroy one tenth of our agricultural wealth, and are more expensive to us than was the yearly cost of the Boer war to England.

We are the victims of pigmy captains of pernicious industries, beside whose gigantic operations such magnates as Carnegie or Mr. Morgan look—in the language of the streets—like thirty cents.

Darwin discovered that human and plant life would perish from the face of the earth were it not for the labours of that humble annelid, commonly known as the angle worm, through whose body the entire superficial soil of the globe passes periodically, and by whose digestive processes it is made amenable for agriculture. The termites subserve the angle worm's efforts by turning over and aerating the soil to an extent very nearly incredible to those who have given no attention to their industry. Our very existence is made possible by the myriad beings for whom our bodies serve as homes and battlefields, and whose dimensions are so minute as to be invisible save under the most powerful microscopes. Ferocious struggles take place within our own tissues between the germs of disease and the white corpuscles of the blood, those brave and sleepless warriors who patrol our veins, and who die by thousands with unreflecting courage in combats with malignant bacteria. When their ranks are thinned, their columns crushed, we succumb helplessly to our invisible foes.

How many of the great and good have fallen victims to those Brinvilliers of the swamps—the anopheles mosquitoes? And a greater number of the young flower of the armies of America and England were slaughtered by the enteric germs carried by flies than fell victims to Boer or Spanish bullets.

How little have we regarded the fly, and yet the facts about this little brother stagger the imagination! It is said to be certain that he came to this country in the Mayflower; but compare his conquests and fertility with that of the Pilgrims. Linnæus said that three flies and the generations that could spring from them could eat a dead horse more rapidly than could a lion, but later knowledge shows that, barring mortality, the number of flies resulting from one female in a summer would be something like seven hundred sextillions, and would in mere bulk outweigh every man, woman, and child on earth. Happily the fly has enemies.

In speaking of these smaller races an idea of their relations to us can only be conveyed by figures; with the larger forms of life the individual may be studied as a type of the race.

We, secure in a conviction of a unique value through the immortality we claim, broadly stigmatize our living fellows as of "the lower orders of life." They are different, it is true, but in what respect lower? Their development is as commensurate with their needs as is ours. The shibboleth of the Socialists —"To each according to his needs, from each according to his abilities," has plainly been the rule with nature. Whatever we boast of achieving has been accomplished as well or better by these lower orders when their necessities have demanded it. Even the Japanese create inferior paper to that made by the wasps, who number among the species the most skilled of carpenters and masons. Who can spin or weave as can the *arachnæ* and their cognate families? The beautiful manufactures of the mollusks—even of the diatoms, invisible save with the microscope—leave us beggared of admiration and envy.

If it be a question of physical qualities let us compare the eye of the eagle, or of a fly, with our own—pit our dull sense of smell with the subtle olfactories of a dog or a wolf—or let one of us test our sense of hearing against that of a mouse or a robin. The albatross loafs in indolent circles about the swiftest of our turbine ships; the porpoise can pass from point to point in his dense element with greater speed than that of our swiftest express engine. The wild goose can do his eighty miles an hour for ten hours without rest. Scare up little Molly Cottontail from your path, and as she flies through the autumn grasses like a light leaf blown before the wind, her delicate and harmonious play of muscular powers leaves our most skilled athletes but clumsy cripples by comparison.

In sight, smell, hearing, speed, strength, grace, and endurance we are immeasurably the inferiors of our dumb brothers. And turning from the material to the spiritual and the ideal, we find that in industry, courage, patriotism, loyalty, fidelity, friendship, chivalry, maternal love, and racial solidity the lower orders have nothing to learn from us. Indeed some races we find advanced in moral progress in certain directions far beyond our most hopeful endeavours.

The needs and laws of their being have developed their morals in differing degree, and the virtues of individuals vary as greatly as among ourselves. Of the characters and ideals of wild creatures we can snatch but brief and tantalizing glimpses; from the larger domestic animals our daily life is too removed to make intimacy possible, but dogs and cats, the free birds, and our caged pets—if considered with a seeing eye—open a door through which we can learn much, though our indolence and stupidity still shut us off from the free community of speech.

Carlyle says: "No nobler feeling than that of admiration for one higher than himself dwells in the breast of man. It is at this hour, and at all hours the unifying influence in man's life. Religion, I find, stands upon it … what, therefore, is loyalty proper, the life breath of all society, but an effluence of hero worship; submissive admiration for the truly great! Society is founded upon hero worship."

Lockhart in his Life of Scot tells of a little pig who conceived a passion of admiration and affection for Scott which much embarrassed the great story teller. This susceptible little porker would lurk about, waiting for Scott's appearance, squealing with joy when he came, and trotting patiently all day at his heels through miles of wandering, proud and contented at merely being allowed to attend on Scott. What was this but Carlyle's hero worship. It is not by the way recorded that any pig ever made a hero of Carlyle. I once had the pleasure of knowing a goose who abandoned his kind for just such a human friendship, and the same love of the admirable is mutual among the animals themselves. A small green paroquet, who lived in the freedom of a bird fancier's room with a canary, was possessed of a passionate admiration for his more gifted companion. His every waking moment was spent in the most touching efforts to imitate the thrilling songs and graceful airiness of his more gifted friend, in no way discouraged by the contumely with which the yellow tenor treated his lumberingly pathetic failures. But there is no more confirmed hero worshipper than your dog. Stevenson says of a dog whom he knew and loved: "It was no sinecure to be Coolin's idol. He was exacting like a rigid parent; and at every sign of levity in the man whom he respected he announced loudly the death of virtue and the proximate fall of the pillars of the earth." And, he adds, "for every station the dog has an ideal to which the master—under pain of derogation—will do wisely to conform. How often has not a cold glance informed me that my dog was disappointed, and how much more gladly would he not have taken a beating than to be thus wounded in the seat of piety."

"Because of all animals the dog is our nearest intimate we know more of his ideals and of his moral traits than of those of the other races. We know that he is vainer than man, singularly greedy of notice, singularly intolerant of ridicule, suspicious like the deaf, jealous to the degree of frenzy."

To quote Stevenson again: "To the dog of gentlemanly feeling theft and falsehood are disgraceful vices. The canine like the human gentleman, demands in his misdemeanours Montaigne's 'je ne sais quoi de genereux!' He is never more than half ashamed of having barked or bitten, and for those faults into which he has been led by a desire to shine before a lady of his race, he retains, even under physical correction, a share of pride. But to be caught lying, if he understands it, instantly uncurls his fleece." "Among dull observers the dog has been credited with modesty. It is amazing how the use of language blunts the faculties of man. That because vain glory finds no vent in words, creatures supplied with eyes have been unable to detect a fault so gross and obvious is amazing. If a small spoiled dog were to be endowed with speech he would prate interminably and still about himself. In a year's time he would have gone far to weary out our love. Hans Christian Andersen, as we behold him in his startling memoirs—thrilling from top to toe with excruciating vanity—scouting the streets for cause of offence—here was your talking dog."

While an egregious, incurable snob the dog is yet the very flower of chivalry. The beggar maid of his kind is sure of as distinguished a consideration from him as is the queen of his race. Indeed he carries his gallantry to so exquisite a point of quixotism that even a female wolf is safe from his teeth. Gratitude is the keynote of his character; to its claims he will subdue even his innate snobbishness, and his devotion to the mysterious laws of his canine etiquette amount to slavishness. "In the elaborate and conscious manners of the dog, moral opinions and the love of the ideal stand confessed. To follow for ten minutes in the street some swaggering canine cavalier is to receive a lesson in dramatic art and the cultured conduct of the body; and in every act and gesture you see him true to a refined conception. For to be a high-mannered and high-minded gentleman, careless, affable, and gay, is the inborn pretension of the dog."

Of all persons now living I personally should most prefer to be enabled to converse freely with that high-bred, subtle-natured lady who follows me in my walks, who shares my meals and lies beside my fire. She has learned with ease to understand my speech, but I, in my gross sluggishness, have neglected to acquire her tongue, and yet how different a place this dull world would appear could I learn all she might tell me. What sights, sounds, and odours, what significances escaping my dull senses, might become open to me! A thousand times I have been aware of her pitying impatience of my slow-wittedness in matters so obvious to her keener intelligence. A whole world lies outside of my apprehension with which she is familiar, and all my life I shall suffer unappeased curiosity as to how she becomes aware of approaching changes in the weather; why a certain part of the wood is taboo. What is it that warns her of a death in my family? Why does a certain good and gentle woman fill her with loathing distrust, and what was the peculiar refinement of insult she received in her puppyhood from the family butcher, which has made it possible for her daily for six years to detect the sound of the butcher's wheels among many others while he is still not in sight, and daily produces in her a rage of resentment that no punishment, no offer of tidbits, has ever been able to allay?

All these things I shall never know. She shares my life, but I, regretfully, protestingly, must stand almost wholly outside of hers.

When we at last seriously take up the great task of articulate communication with the animals, a new world will swim into our ken beside which the discovery of America will seem but an unimportant event. Half of the unexplained puzzles of science will be solved with ease, and whole departments of knowledge as yet undreamed of will be opened to our astonished understandings.

Perhaps by our little dumb brothers we are still compassionately reckoned as the deaf and blind giant.

AUGUST 5.
Fever Dreams.

A thousand times the great clock's heart has beat—
A thousand, thousand times,
And ever at the hours the sudden, sweet,
Low, unexpected ringing of the chimes
Tells how the night doth slowly pass away.
The hissing snow fell through the air all day,
But with the dark did cease—
I hear the shivers of the frozen trees.
The night-lamp's gleam—though weak the flame and small—
Casts shadows giant tall
That to the ceiling crawl—
The cap-frill of the sleeping nurse doth fall
And nod this way and that against the wall.
Quiet the great dark house, and deeply sleep they all—
They held me fast, they could not hear the call
That I heard always—chill the winds did blow—
The skies were dark—the ways were white with snow—
He did not call—I wandered to think so.
But now they sleep, I will arise and go.
They think him dead, but his sweet voice I know.
I stretch my hands, my heart beats hard—his voice is sweet and
        low,
But muffled by the weight of earth, and hath a note of woe—
He calls to me: I cannot stay; I must arise and go—
I step out on the floor—
(How loud that nurse doth snore)
But I softly close the door.
I quickly pass from the outer door.
It is very, very cold!—
But he will me closely fold
With a tender clasping arm,
And still my deep alarm—
In his heart I shall be warm!
The snow is smooth as glass.
I scarcely leave a foot-print as I pass—
It is very cold, and the way is long, alas!
And they have buried him deep, so deep under the frozen grass.
It was cruel to bury him so deep;
He was not dead, he was only asleep—

He was not dead; it makes me weep
To think he is in this frozen ground—
Why does the moon whirl round and round!
My head is dizzy; I'm faint and ill—
Will no one make the moon stand still?
The foolish moon whirls round and round—
What is it that the pine trees know,
That they rustle and whisper together so?
Someone was buried under the snow
More than a thousand years ago!—
My long black shadow runs by my side.
Was it I, or my love that died
And was buried deeply under the snow
So many hundred years ago?
Oh! *how* can I reach him under the ground?
I am burning with fire, my head turns round.
He does not call me, I hear no sound—
Ah!—will no one come to me? I'm all alone,
The nurse does not hear, she's as deaf as a stone,
The walls of the grave together have grown,
The dead man lies still and makes no moan,
They have left me here with this corpse alone—!
His golden hair is tarnished with rust;
His eyes have withered and fallen to dust—
His subtle, secret, amber eyes;
The worms might have spared those amber eyes—
His lips are grey with dust and sunken;
His heart is cold, and his cheeks are shrunken—
He must be dead, so still he lies!

I lay in my bed and he called to me,
They held me, but it might not be
That we should rest so far apart,
And we have lain here, heart to heart,
Since I came out across the snow
More than a thousand years ago.

SEPTEMBER 7.
A Misunderstood Moralist.

Mary R—— was telling us to-day the details of Zola's accidental death—if it was an accident. There are a few, she tells me, who whisper privately that the enemies he made by "Lourdes" and "Rome" are of the sort who wait long and patiently, and strike hard, and strike at the back when the time of vengeance comes. That sounds rather sensational, and certainly the general public have heard no such suggestion.

The story of the death-chamber is like a chapter from one of his own books, and one can't but feel how gruesome and vivid he would have made the account of the tragedy could he have recorded it.

It's rather odd how the multitude still judge Zola at the rating of twenty years since, before he had developed the meaning of his methods and proved himself one of the greatest of the moral teachers.

It was certainly as long ago as that when a battered, grimy copy of "Nana" drifted by some swirl of chance into my youthful hands. I was quite old enough to realize that my pastors and masters would be convulsed with horror did they at all suspect what I was at, but being in those days as omnivorous as Lamb—"Shaftesbury was not too genteel for me, nor Jonathan Wild too low"—everything on which a hand could be laid passed into my greedy mental maw, from Locke "On the Human Understanding" to the novels of the Duchess, and I had intelligence enough not to chatter about every book I opened.

I remember with perfect vividness the moral revelation given me by the chapter descriptive of the drunken orgie in Nana's rooms, where they wound up the gaieties of the evening by the spirited jest of pouring the champagne into the piano. In a flash was made clear to me what I had never previously suspected, that vice was tedious and unamusing!

Until that moment I had accepted in perfect good faith the insistence of the moralists upon the delicious, exciting, irresistible nature of vice, which, though deplorable in its eventual effects, was too agreeable to be refrained from unless fortified by either religion or the choicest collection of moral maxims.

We were the contented owners, at that same period, of a large engraving of a popular painting entitled "The Prodigal Son"; one of those pictures supposed to have a "good moral" and help silently, in season and out of season, to point towards virtue like a sign at the crossroads. The engraving was divided into three parts, like a triptych; the central, and by far the largest portion, showed the famous ne'er-do-weel prodigalling with all his might in a sort of lordly pleasure dome, all columns and sweeping curtains and steps, open to the sunshine on every side, and decorated with the most expensive cut flowers. A meal, which plainly deserved to be called by no meaner name than a banquet, was toward, and the naughty young gentleman, bedecked in velvet and soothed by the music of viols, was feasting amid a medley of young ladies of the most dazzling physical charms, all attired in those sketchy toilets which have no visible means of support, and which allow the artist to prove his inexhaustible talent for drawing arms and busts. So vivacious and sumptuous was this scene that at first one hardly noticed the narrow panels to right and left, in one of which the profuse prodigal was on a subsequent occasion dining en famille with the swine, and later journeying toward forgiveness and veal.

The moralists, from Isaiah down, have so dearly loved to show their talent for drawing arms and busts. The delineation of vice always usurps all the foreground of the canvas. According to them, the broad road is unfailing in its crops of flowers, the wine is always red in the cup, "with beaded bubbles winking at the brim." The frisky enchantresses are without exception young and charming. The reverse of the picture is depressingly bleak—by way of proper dramatic contrast, perhaps, though to any one less austere than a moralist it would seem unintelligent to point out that in one direction all was gay, brilliant, and agreeable, yet one must follow the gloomy, tedious, and unpleasant road in order to find some intangible spiritual satisfaction, which to youthful and ardent minds seems drearily remote, and unsatisfying when reached. Besides it really isn't true. Life as a matter of fact is certainly more agreeable when one behaves one's self decently. Nothing was ever more blatantly untrue than the cynical proverb which declares that everything pleasant is either indigestible, expensive, or immoral. But the mind of youth is almost touchingly credulous. It rarely questions the accuracy of the descriptions of the moralists, who claim to be experts, though instinctively it develops a necessity for experimenting a little with those forbidden sweets of which it has heard so much praise.

Until I read "Nana" it never occurred to me to question that vice was in itself agreeable, since I had never heard aught to the contrary; but that champagne poured into the piano washed away the conviction forever. It seemed so squalid, so unimaginative, so dull; and all the vice I have observed since has shared its lack of charm. I found that the broad road had no patent on flowers and sunshine, that dishonesty nine times out of ten failed of returns at all commensurate with the energy devoted to it; that loose behaviour was nearly always noisome and fatiguing; that the prodigal, instead of being a beautiful young person in velvet, generally had a red nose and a waist, and borrowed from his acquaintances, and that the enchantresses had not nearly as good figures as the painters credited them with, and as a rule had no real feeling for soap and water. The truth is that all forms of vice are for the most part not only repulsive but intolerably unamusing, and Zola was the first of the moralists who had the courage to be original and speak disrespectfully of it.

September 10.
The Pleasures of Pessimism.

A man who took me in to dinner Wednesday night said, pityingly,

"You seem to be a pessimist. Why is that? Are you unhappy?"

That sort of remark is a shot between wind and water, and leaves one speechless. I crossly denied being an ——ist of any sort, and changed the subject.

Possibly he was led to his banal personality by some remark I had made, of the sort that is commonly called cynical because it is true.

The optimists have a theory that those who don't take the same view of life as themselves must therefore be unhappy. It's an amazing conclusion. They seem to have no idea how the pessimists enjoy their own sense of superiority. It is as if the blind should say to the man with eyes: "How unhappy you must be to see things just as they are. Now I can imagine them to be anything I please!"

The man with eyes could, of course, only smile; it being obviously impossible to discuss such a proposition.

The believers in personal immortality labour under the same curious illusion apparently. They are so sorry for those who don't believe in it, and imagine them frightened at the thought of death. To their minds the universe is inconceivable without their presence, seemingly forgetful of the fact that it got on quite well before they came. It is rather an imposing bit of egotism, after all. It rises to the level of grandeur.

Catholics, I know, have the same pity and astonishment about the state of mind of Protestants that the optimists feel for pessimists, the religious for the unbelieving. Each thinks the heretic in parlous state and fancies he must be secretly disturbed by it, when of a truth the heretic is simply amused by this anxiety for his welfare, and cheerfully certain of his own superiority.

SEPTEMBER 18.
Moral Pauperism.

M——, who has, with some flourish of trumpet and tuck of drum, gone over to Rome, is the daughter of a Presbyterian minister, I am told, and, what is odder still, is a very clever and humorous creature. One can discount the parson and the cleverness, but a *humorous* Protestant 'verting is more difficult to understand.

I tried hard to get some explanation from her as to her point of view, but she was entirely vague. Fancy—she has a patron saint, beads, etc.! One can only gape.

Very probably every one is at birth—no matter what the environment—either Catholic or Protestant by nature. To many it is an absolute necessity that someone else should furnish their spiritual and mental support. With these, no matter how frequently one sets them on their feet their knees will give under them; no matter how often one starts them in spiritual business one has eventually to come again to the rescue. To such an one the perpetual supervision and personal tyranny of the Catholic Church must seem deliciously comfortable and protecting. No wonder they are drawn to it across all barriers.

To the born Protestant such bondage is as intolerable as spoon feeding and a wheeled chair would be to an athlete. Whatever the moral or mental situation may be he must deal with it for himself—must stand on his own feet—use his own moral muscles. Neither can ever understand the other. Their whole attitude toward life is directly opposed. Each seeks what his nature demands.

SEPTEMBER 30.
On a Certain Lack of Humour in Frenchmen.

The book-club has eliminated Marcel Prevost's "Mariage de Julianne" as too naughty for our perusal—though not until we had *all* read it, to see how undesirable it was.

To what H—— calls my "robust nature" it seemed merely deliciously funny and human, and I am not fond of French fiction as a rule. Most of it leaves in my mind only a sense of dreary nastiness—a sort of more closely knit Hall Caine-ism, with his sloppiness of style left out. Yet a good many of one's contemporaries profess to find French fiction vastly superior to English literature of the same sort: to find Balzac a greater artist than Thackeray; but those who make this assertion are, I find, generally lacking in humour and imagination themselves, and therefore blind to a whole side of life. They, of nature, think marionettes liker life than beings of flesh and blood. Balzac's dry, minute descriptions give them an impression of reality. To hear that a man had a red nose, had iron-grey hair growing thin on top, and that his bottle-green trousers wrinkled at the knees, gives them the sensation that Balzac is presenting them with "a slice of life"—not being aware, it would seem, that this might be equally truthful a description of a wax figure at Madame Tussaud's. Such matters as these are not the essentials that differentiate a man from his fellows.

Henry James thinks this elaboration of detail is Balzac's "strongest gift" and adds, "Dickens often sets a figure before us with extraordinary vividness, but the outline is fantastic and arbitrary—we but half believe in it." It seems to me that James has, like Balzac, but a half developed sense of life. He too is meticulous in his efforts to make one see and feel what he wishes to convey, because he only half feels and sees it himself; though he is concerned rather with emotions than objects, and in spite of the labour and care expended by each, but a shadowy impression remains. Dickens can dash in a few broad, half caricatured lines of a portrait because the figure he wishes to show is so vivid to his own eye he feels it only necessary to indicate it broadly to make others recognize it. Uncle Pumblechook in "Great Expectations" is suggested, as far as written description goes, in merest outline—"A large, hard-breathing, middle-aged, slow man, with a mouth like a fish, dull staring eyes, and sandy hair standing upright on his head"—yet after half a page of his conversation and his welcome to Pip at the funeral, "breathing sherry and crumbs," one needs no more. The man lives and moves. One knows him inside and out.

James speaks again of Balzac's "choking one with his bricks and mortar," and thinks his houses, his rooms, his towns, "unequalled for vividness of presentation, of realization." To an imaginative reader they are as dry and superfluous as a real-estate agent's pamphlets; one has a sense of the author's heavy straining effort to make the places palpable to his own mental vision. It is the weary iteration of the bore, who having no imagination can leave nothing to that of his hearer.

Dickens somewhere describes a room merely by telling how the winking fire was reflected in every smooth object. The fire winks cheerily; the pewters winking dully, as if afraid of being suspected of not seeing the joke; the furniture twinkling slyly from every polished point, etc., etc., in Dickens's well-known fashion of pursuing a happy fancy round and round. There is not one word of catalogue of the room's contents, yet it remains forever as vivid in the reader's memory as a chamber with which one is intimately familiar.

Bulwer says that "French nature is not human nature," and if human nature was necessarily the Anglo-Saxon conception of life it would be true. Nothing so points French heterogeneousness from ourselves as the attitude of our two chosen masters of the novel, Balzac and Thackeray. Not a gleam of humour ever irradiates for a moment the pages of the former. A mere glimmer would make impossible his story of the young man who endeavours to compromise a pretty woman, whose refusal to yield to his dishonourable suggestions so puzzles and disgusts him that he can only explain her coldness as being the probable results of some secret but mortal disease!... A lover abducts a reluctant fair by mingled force and stratagem, and attempts to brand her with hot irons; accompanying this gentle gallantry with the mummeries of a thirteenth-century Inquisition. This picturesque proof of devotion so touches the lady that she promptly grovels in an agony of affection for this chivalrous admirer....

All this is told with perfect gravity, the author having not the smallest suspicion of its absurdity—and yet there be actually Anglo-Saxons who solemnly announce that Balzac knew human nature to its depths. French nature, perhaps; certainly not ours....

A spinster lives twenty years in a family, all of whose members she venomously hates, and not one of them suspect her unselfish devotion until she aids in humiliating them and wrecking their fortunes.... Madame Hulot is a saint, and yet at fifty years of age offers her person to a repulsive scoundrel in order to provide a marriage portion for her daughter; Balzac evidently considering this one of her noblest acts.

The point at which one finds the widest divergence of the French and English attitudes toward life is in the essay made by each of these chosen spokesmen to show us the adventuress. Taine, who honestly tried to see English literature from English eyes and interpret it to his countrymen, breaks down entirely when he reaches this angle of vision.

He says: "There is a personage unanimously recognized as Thackeray's masterpiece, Becky Sharp…. Let us compare her with a similar personage of Balzac in 'Les Parents Pauvre,' Valerie Marneff. The difference in the two works will exhibit the difference in the two literatures"—and they do indeed.

Valerie to the English reader is the old commonplace, stereotyped adventuress of the melodrama. One can imagine none save those as vile and stupid as herself being deceived by such a greedy, outrageous creature. The descriptions of her looks and behaviour smack of the unhumorous shilling shocker. She gives glances from beneath "her long eyelids like the glare of cannon seen through smoke!" … and again "her eyes flashed like daggers."

Such figures of speech sound like the pompous rhodomontade of a Laura Jean Libby, yet Taine quotes them with much admiration.

Becky, Taine finds incomprehensible. He complains that Thackeray "degrades her" when he laughingly reveals her secret vulgar shifts. Also he is resentful because her carefully built schemes crumble one by one like houses of cards, being ignorant, apparently, of that choice old utilitarian proverb as to Honesty being the best policy, founded upon a very general observation that the same cleverness and energy employed by adventurers in their nefarious schemes pays a far higher rate of interest when turned to legitimate pursuits.

The half affectionate, half contemptuous humour with which her creator regards Becky shocks Taine. With his French passion for logical completeness he cannot comprehend that Thackeray's vision for truth should make him capable of admitting and admiring that arch-adventuress's good qualities,— the very qualities of her defects which made her career of deception possible. The consistent monster Valerie could delude no one, while Becky's patience, gaiety, and good nature made Rawdon Crawley's devotion plausible, and forced even Lord Steyne, who recognized her baseness, after a fashion to respect and like her, and consent to be used by her, until—by a fundamental impulse of womanliness—"she admired her husband standing there, grand, brave, victorious," above the prostrate body of her seducer. It is that same underlying womanliness in Becky—of which Valerie lacked even an intimation—which makes her human and real. Its absence leaves Valerie incredible and shadowy.

Take again Lear and Goriot. The latter's children have no excuse whatever for their crimes of greed and selfishness. They are grotesque succubi, while the astounding wickedness of Regan and Goneril is made credible by Lear's own violent foolishness and vanity. His tempestuous senility is of the sort that wakes the blindest revolt of youth, which is always restless under the dominance of age, a restlessness likely to deepen to cruelty when age is unrestrained by wisdom or dignity.

A Frenchman once complained to me bitterly of the comic porter in Macbeth, who comes grumbling to unlock the gate so soon after the horror of the murder of Duncan. To him the touch of comedy seemed vulgar and inept. It was impossible to make him understand how to the Anglo-Saxon mind this veracious touch of comedy jostling tragedy but heightened the dramatic poignancy of the play. This incapacity to see the humorous contrasts of life and character is generally characteristic of youth with its narrow inexperience of realities, and the French and the unhumorous of our own race seem never to outgrow this juvenility.

OCTOBER 15.
The Value of a Soul.

I wonder if anyone will ever muster up sufficient courage to write the true history of the ferocious egotism engendered in the human heart by a belief in human immortality. The most cynical might well shrink from the sorrowful task. Self-preservation, supposedly the first law of nature, is but a feeble instinct when placed in comparison, for motherhood, patriotism, sexual love; a thousand minor passions will induce human beings to abandon their inheritance in the warm precincts of the cheerful day, but all that a man hath, and all that his friends, and the wife of his bosom, and the children of his loins have, will he give for that wretched little flyspecked object he calls his soul.

Buckle rather shocked a pious world when he announced that in many cases the best kings, considered from the point of view of their private characters, made the worst rulers; but all history is loud with this truth. The moment anyone in power began to consider the question of his soul with seriousness, tears and blood soon began to flow. A ruler who had strong secular tendencies usually had some sort of consideration for human happiness, but one who turned his mind to what was called "higher things" waded through the wretchedness of those in his power with noble insouciance. Henri IV., who was cheerfully indifferent as to whether he heard preaching by parsons or the mass of priests, provided he might have Paris for his capital, quieted the fratricidal religious conflicts of France and made life happy for his subjects; and Henry II. of England, who was the only one of the Angevin Kings entirely unconcerned about his immortal future, did more for England than any ruler since Alfred, and would have trebled those wise secular benefits had à-Becket and the rest of the troublesome clergy permitted it.

I have been roused to these moral generalizations by Quiller-Couch's novel, "Hetty Wesley." It's a poignant book.

Hetty was the sister of the founders of Methodism, and Quiller-Couch has availed himself, in writing the book, of the letters and papers of that remarkable family. He has told his tale very simply and with an artist's comprehension and sympathy, setting down nothing in malice and leaving the reader to draw his own inferences.

The picture of that damp Epworth Rectory where Charles and John were born (two out of the ten living children, several others had died early) makes the Brontë Parsonage, over which it is the fashion to shiver, seem like an amiable idyl by contrast. Samuel Wesley, the father, was passionately religious. The first of his concerns was the saving of his own soul for immortal happiness, the second was the saving of as many other like heirs to bliss as possible, and a part of this second ambition implied the training of his sons for the ministry. In pursuit of these ends he sacrificed the comfort and happiness of his wife and seven lovely daughters with a ruthless persistency and consistency that would be incredible did we not have his own complacent writings in testimony thereto.

The sons found his example worthy of imitation, it appears. Of late, apropos of the Wesley Centennial, one has heard much of John Wesley, of his tangled love affairs and his amazing marriage, and one can't but be conscious of a secret liking for that tempestuous termagant, Mrs. John, because that she after a fashion avenged those eight unlucky kinswomen whose lives he so complacently sucked dry to nourish his religious aspirations.

One has wondered, when reading them, if those meek and loyal addresses from the scaffold, made to Henry VIII. by the innocent victims of his bloodthirstiness, could have been genuine documents. They contradict all one knows of human nature in their humble acquiescence and submissive affection; but here in this book we have Hetty Wesley's own tender appeal to her father—a father who had ruthlessly cast her into a lifelong hell—to forgive what he called a sin, really only a girl's generous foolish mistake, and we have also his answer. An answer which would have made even Tudor Henry blush for its cruelty. One could almost wish that there was somewhere an immortal part of Samuel Wesley, burning eternally in the knowledge of himself as he really was. Mrs. John Wesley saves us the need of wishing that Hetty's brother had a soul.

After all, this is but one of thousands of grim stories of human beings trampling upon the lives and hearts of their fellows in the endeavour to achieve for themselves an infinity of bliss. To my heretical mind such behaviour for such an end seems inexpressibly sordid, vulgar, and selfish. I at least prefer to be one with the dumb beasts that perish, but who pass away knowing that no creature has ever suffered a pang in order that they may have saved their souls alive.

A Grateful Spaniard.

Time is not long enough for me
  To hate mine enemy perfectly,
But God is of infinite mercy and he
  To Time has added Eternity.

OCTOBER 16.
Bores.

I reproached J—— last night for sending me to dinner with E——. "This is the third time you have done it," I grumbled, "and it is just twice too often. None of the other women will talk to him, and because I treat him decently you take advantage of my good nature."

"Oh, but my dear," she countered impishly, "you know you are so juicy with bores!"

Of course, that was true, though there is nothing I envy more than the courage of ruthlessness—one of the first laws of social self-preservation. I am always the helpless prey of bores. They drink as they choose from my "sacred fount," though it is shallow enough, heaven knows! for me to need all its contents for myself. If this condition of affairs arose from good nature I should not be ashamed of it, but it is all sheer cowardliness. My imagination is so vivid that I can feel the corroding humiliation of neglect and indifference to the poor souls as if it were being applied to my own skin, and I labour on, crying protests inwardly, rather than free myself by a moment of brutality.

"Tell bores who waste my time and me" that the best hours of my life have been burned in their dull fires. Again and again have I lost my opportunity to seek the friendship of some adorably amusing creature while sweating to pull the oar that was the bore's own proper task.

This indolent cowardice enfeebles me in a dozen ways; makes it impossible for me to train my dogs for fear of hurting their feelings, and to discharge a servant costs me a white night and a *fausse digestion*. It is not kindliness, it is only that I feel their discomfort more than they do themselves.

November 7.
Emotions and Oxydization.

H—— told a curious story last night of the bobstay on his yacht, which time after time rusted, broke, and betrayed him at critical moments of racing. Replacing with the best material and by the best workmen was futile, though all the rest of the wire rigging remained intact. It seemed a "hoodoo" until it was discovered to be due to oxydization from a bolt which touched a copper plate on the stem. F—— said it was easy to see how, before the chemical action of steel and copper were understood, the most sensible and logical mind might be driven to attribute such a thing to witchcraft, and it occurred to me that perhaps when we know more of the chemistry of psychology, many of our emotional puzzles will be more easily solved. Jealousy, anger, suspicion, ingratitude, it will then be easy to correct by some simple act of insulation. We know that many evil moral tendencies are caused by pressure upon certain portions of the brain, and my own personal experience and long observation makes me confident that half the baser passions are due to acidity in the blood. It makes one slow to indulge one's emotions when one realizes they may simply be the result of a lack of a therapeutic alkali. With such a conviction one will generally wait for the slower and more balanced action of reason.

What a great alteration would take place in the history of the world if it could be rewritten from the point of view of what the doctors describe as "the gouty acid diathesis."

Bess of Hardwicke's marital troubles, which convulsed all England, and even drew Elizabeth and Burleigh into the turmoil, were due entirely to the unhappy Earl's gout, as no one can doubt after reading his letters. Charles V. was driven from his throne by it, and Napoleon's gout lost him the battle of Leipsic and set his feet in "slippery places." Henry VIII.'s shoes were not slashed without reason, and Pitt was lost to England when she most needed him by the same agent. These are but a few of the notorious examples, but how many wars, revolutions, massacres, had their origin in that same corroding oxydization of the spirit of man we will probably never fully determine.

NOVEMBER 10.
Abelard to Heloise.

     Dear Sister in Christ:
God send you peace from Heaven!
I would that to your restless heart
His blessed peace was given,
And that you found
In contemplation of His love
Balm for that wound
That ever frets you sore.
'Twere meet you wore
Much sack cloth,
And with scourge and fasting drove
This passion from your soul....
Christ's Bride thou art;
Therefore give Him the whole.
I charge thou keep'st back not any part
Of His just due to spend upon a worm....
Nay, woman! would'st thou bring on me a curse
For that I stand between thy soul and God?...
Thy love for me is but a thing perverse.
Cast it forth from thee, or a heavy rod
May prove that God is still a jealous God.
But that you are a woman, and infirm
Of will and purpose, I should say
Some bitter words to purge you of this sin!
Natheless each day
I painful penance do
For that 'twas I who led you first astray—
(For which great sin may He my soul assoil!)
And wrestle mightily each night in prayer
That Christ may yet your stubborn heart subdue
To His sweet will, and—the sharp fret and coil
Of earth cast forth—He then may enter in
To find a garnished chamber, and an altar fair....
—Nay, now, bethink you!
Love like yours is grievous sin,
And the time wasteth swift toward death.
All love is but a breath

Which clouds the glass that we see darkly through—
When you to Heaven shall win
And there see face to face your risen Lord,
Wilt know 'twas but the hot fume of a word
Spake by a devil, dimmed your earthly glass....
In essence love is sin!—
Save only love of God.
It is a gin,
Set by the Evil One to snare the feet
Of those who haste toward Heaven,
By its false likeness to the spiritual love,
And by it man is driven
Down the steep slope to Hell.
'Tis thus when sanctioned by the Church; how then
Of love like thine, which is accursed of men,
And doubly cursed by God?...
Last night in dreams I trod
Up the long windings of the heavenly stair,
And heard the angels singing loud and sweet,
And neared the gate, when sudden both my feet
Were caught amid the tangles of thy hair,—
Spread like a cruel web across my path,—
In which I struggled, mad with woe and wrath,
And could not free me; so at last I fell,
Stumbling and plunging down to blackest Hell,
Wherein I cursed the hour I saw thy face,
And most I cursed the hour, the day, the place
When thou didst give me love....
Waking then, I strove
For holier thoughts, and could at last forgive
The wrong thou didst me.
But no more, I prithee, vex me with thy tale
Of love. It wearieth me, and henceforth I must live
In larger peace, or I may not prevail
Within the Schools
Against the babbling of the narrow fools
Who blindly are withstanding my new light
Upon the Divine Essence's nature, and my clasp
Of the ringed Trinitarian mysteries. Matters your slight
Woman's comprehension may not grasp....
Farewell. Neglect not prayer.

Heloïse to Abelard.

My good Lord Abbot:—But this once
I speak, and then no more.
I must not 'gainst the lore
Of the great Schools
Set my weak cries
For warmth and life and love.
The snow now lies
Deep round the Paraclete,
Where from my pale nuns rise
In never ceasing chant of nones and primes
Incense of prayers to ease the need of God
For broken contrite hearts and dropping tears.
And sometimes I have fears
That each one wears
'Neath her long habit
As sad a heart as mine,
For in their eyes,
Which each unto the skies
Lifts many times each day,
I see desire for love,
A gift they pray
From God, since man gives not
That which they need.
I watch them from my carven chair,
While lingering on a bead,
And add, beneath my hood,
Beads to my rosary of tears
To think how good
To each 'twould seem to change
This Latin drone and censer's clank
For the dear homely noise
Around the hearth
Of little girls and boys—
For all these weary prayers
The daily household cares
For some tired labourer
Who earned their bread.
Oh, little hands and feet!—

There is no room
Within this cloistered tomb
Wherein we worship God,
For one dear curly head.

———————————————

Sometimes at prayers
A vision seems to rise—
Borne on an air
Mayhap that blows from Hell.
And then I see the great Lord Jove
And all His mighty peers
Who ruled so many years
Above the ancient heavens,
Dwindle, and fade, and pass away,
And only Love remains—
I see the doctors of the ancient schools,
Great Egypt's sages, those who made the rules
Of wisdom in the Academe,
Fade also like a dream;
All their wise thoughts grow foolishness
And all their learning turns to dust,
And only Love remains
Forever young, forever wise and great,
And in the time to come
I see the same strong fate
Seize on our Mighty God
Who binds us in his chains,
And makes our love a sin
To drive our souls to Hell,
He too, with all his doctors
Fades—and only Love remains
Forever and forever. Fare you well.

———————————————

November 30.
Yumei Mujitsu.

The Japanese possess a delightful word—Yumei Mujitsu—which signifies "Having-the-Name-but-not-the-Reality." They use it to express certain assumptions—such, for example, as the claim of the Mikado's descent from the Sun Goddess, which, like the formulæ of Algebra, achieve desired results though they recognize that in itself it has no existence. How valuable such a word would be to express the attitude of the Sentimentalist regarding a coloured man named Booker Washington, much discussed of late.

Now if there is one creature more than a saint whom I fear and distrust it is the Sentimentalist, whom Hawthorne pungently characterizes as "that steel machine of the Devil's own make." The ruthless heartlessness of the Sentimentalist would be unbelievable if one had not seen it with one's own eyes. Take, for example, the Abolitionists. To gratify their own emotions they caused the death of a million men, the infliction of wounds and pain that make the imagination shudder, and all that long succeeding anguish of a people—the grief, the poverty, humiliation, and despair that burned itself indelibly upon the hearts of those who shared it.

Stevenson—that misunderstood moralist now chiefly remembered as a story teller!—put his finger upon the enigma of the Sentimentalist's cruelty:

"Everywhere some virtue cherished or affected, everywhere some decency of thought or carriage, everywhere the ensign of man's ineffectual goodness:— Ah, if I could show you these! if I could show you these men and women all the world over … clinging in the brothel and on the scaffold to some rag of honour, the poor jewel of their souls!… They may seek to escape and yet they cannot … they are condemned to some nobility, all their lives the desire of good is at their heels, the implacable hunter…. To touch the heart of his mystery we find in him the thought of something owing to himself, to his neighbour, to his God."

The Sentimentalist, along with all his kind, is hunted by that implacable need of virtue. To satisfy it he seizes upon the wrongs done by others, and in his hot denunciation of another's sin, in his clamour for its punishment, he experiences the warm ennobling glow of personal merit.

The pietist will meticulously perform rites and ceremonies in this same need to soothe the imperious call within him for some justification of his life. Having washed and bowed and recited, his sins of practice trouble him but little—those genuflections have made his balance good in the book of virtue. But the Sentimentalist cannot content himself with pale ceremonies. He is by instinct devouring and bloody, but his soul cringes before his inward monitor. By fierce denunciation of the sins he has no mind to he can soothe his desire to inflict pain in perfect content, upborne by a consciousness of his own righteousness. Torquemada was a type, John Brown of Ossawatamie another; both were criminal paranoics tortured by desire for blood and for self-justification. Real goodness does not stimulate the Sentimentalist's emotions —it gives no opportunity for the outcries that warm his heart with a consciousness of rectitude.

The Boer war was a great opportunity for the American Sentimentalist. Protesting against the suppression of a Republic, he could forget his own suppression of the Confederate Republic and of the nascent government of the Philippines. Execrating the burning of farmhouses in the Veldt, he could ignore the track of smoking desolation that marked Sherman's march through Georgia or Sheridan's raid in Virginia. Criticism of British greed for gold kept him cheerfully superior to the contrast of the gift of fifteen millions and the patient labour spent by the English to repatriate the Boer and start him again in life, with the protest he and his kind made against General Grant's willingness to leave to the Southern soldier his starved horse as a means of reaching his ruined home.

Conscience, demanding of the Sentimentalist the bread of uprightness, he prodigally offers it a stone upon which to break its gnawing teeth.

The African brother has long been one of the most valued of the Sentimentalist's resources. Passionately generous demands for the negro's equality have made it possible for him to cordially and contentedly insult and oppress his white fellow countrymen.

It is in this relation that the Sentimentalists find Booker Washington so greatly to their taste. Washington, innocent of their purposes, of course is an admirable and sensible man, who has established an excellent school for the young people of his race. A school far wiser and more merciful in conception than any attempt made by the negrophiles to benefit their protégés, and all honour is due this enlightened ex-slave for his own astonishing progress and his generous sharing of his fruitful labours with his own people. The Sentimentalist professes to find in it "something godlike," a "touch of the divine," as one of them recently characterized what is, reduced to simple facts, the establishing of an industrial school for negroes by a negro.

DECEMBER 1.
The Real Thing.

The man who has educated the negro, the man who has had in him really a touch of the divine, would never appeal to the Sentimentalist.

Booker Washington, very properly, of course, lives and lives well upon the results of his school. He has claimed from the rich, and justly has received, lavish aid for his enterprise. He dresses well, lives amply, travels in comfort, is entertained by Royalty and Chief Magistrates, and with his family, is put beyond even a chance of narrow means by his sympathizers' lavishness. But who heeds the man who has really educated the negro? What crowned head or President entertains the small farmer in rough brogans and faded jeans, who sweats over his hoe in the cotton and tobacco fields, or in the steaming rice and sugar-cane swamps, and who has in forty years spent more than a hundred millions upon the education of the negro? This is the man, and the son of the man who turned heart-brokenly home on the begrudged horse to fields overgrown and laid waste—fields to which his conquerors, unlike the English, contributed no seeds or implements or stock—and from that land he has wrung by the hard labour of his hands that hundred millions which has been spent in educating his ex-slave.

He has lived hardly, in dingy, decaying houses, he has eaten of the coarsest, he has known no beauty or grace, and but scant comfort, he has been clothed in the plainest, he has politically known little but injury and contempt from the larger and wealthier half of his country, and worst of all he has seen his sons grow to manhood but partially and inadequately equipped with learning, because so large a portion of their birthright must be shared in the teaching of the negro in whose name he had been plundered and slaughtered.

The touching point of the story is that it has all been done without any consciousness of special merit. The duty was to be done, and was done without trumpets or drums. Such silent, patient, unreflecting, unadvertised goodness would, of course, never appeal to the Sentimentalist. If he could be brought to see it 'twould merely disturb his self-satisfaction.

It is only to the fantastic mind of a heretic that its meaning appeals, only the heart of a cynic is touched by the instinctive heroism of the white man of the South.

DECEMBER 15.
"Oh, Eloquent, Just, and Mighty Death."

I am just home from a meeting of one of those literary clubs we American women so much affect, in the absence of any masculine society, and we have been talking about Stevenson as the poet most typical of the mind of the nineteenth century. It was all that delicious welter in the sentimentalities of the domestic affections which any assemblage of females finds it impossible to avoid; and we read aloud to one another—with the *vox humana* lilt turned on—all those decidedly dull little lyrics in the "Child's Garden of Verses," and came away with just that moist brightness of the eye, that wistful, tender "mother-smile," which was correct of the occasion.

I say *we*, but of course my wicked old eyes were as hard as horn, yet, thank heaven! my unruly tongue uttered not a note out of tune with the Domestic Symphony. Who will say that social slappings have taught me nothing? Even I can be daunted by the unhappy silences that so often greet my blurted comments, and by the soft rustles of relief that respond to the rising of some gentle lady, who will obliquely but certainly crush me with her pious phrases, that throb with the warm sweetness of the dear old human platitudes, and which are rewarded by applause which politely accentuates my disgrace.... Oh, amiable and philosophic white page! To you I can be a tiresome and protesting bore, sure of no strictures in your silence. Here I can unpack my heart with words, unrebuked. Here I can whisper safely my suspicion that dear R. L. S. himself would have been consumed with cheerful amusement at our gentle comments upon his doughty spirit.

The world says all sorts of absurd things about Stevenson. Some one the other day called him "an unquenchable Calvinist"!—He who was all pagan and Roman. The Calvinist was the European most subdued by the Semitic beliefs, most merged into Oriental preconceptions of life.

Certainly the European mind in its natural state faced its consciousness of existence with no preconceived theories. Its attitude was that of the child. It found itself face to face with a great, astonishing, beautiful universe, and asked itself what it must think of this universe; how use its opportunities therein. The child stumbled into a thousand infantile delusions and misconceptions, but its eyes were unclouded, its intelligence good. He soon discovered that though many things were pleasant, these pleasant things, when used indiscreetly, had a hidden potentiality of pain. With this second discovery, however—being a wise child—came no foolish horror of all pleasant things; only an illumination as to the value of moderation.

The phenomena of age, death, and decay left the child serious, but not depressed. These were not pleasant things, admittedly; but since they appeared inevitable, there was plainly no use in attempting to escape them. The proper attitude toward such solemnities was a manly courage, a brave submission. In any case, the child concluded, with all the sufferings, contradictions, and puzzling inequalities of existence, at least for all those called upon to face these griefs, there remained some small space of clear, warm, beautiful life; sunshine, food, love, and—more and better than all— that tingling, exquisite quiver of the senses which he agreed to call by the divine name of Beauty. He saw that the pains, the joys, the growth and blight, decay and extinction, were not of his lot only, but were shared by all his surroundings. Feeling himself alone neither in his opportunities nor his inevitable doom, he accepted his fate with the courageous calm, the uncomplaining resignation, of his fellow-creatures. He lived and he died as unresentfully as did the summer leaves, whose season of existence was so much briefer than his own.

His kinship with encompassing nature was so close that it touched him on every side. He became as aware of the souls of all things about him as he was aware of his own. He felt a similar spirit of life in the trees of the forest, the stones of the mountains, in the sea winds, in the brooks, the rivers and their reeds. He guessed at their names, their loves, their histories, as one guesses at those of unknown passers-by travelling the same road. Out of these speculations arose all his arts, his poetry, his legends, and his myths. When the moon stooped toward the western hills she leaned in a passion like his own toward youth and desire. The blood of a slain love became visible to him as it returned to the upper air in dim, faint-scented blossoms, bearing written on their purple leaves the plaintive *ai! ai!* of her left mourning for dead beauty. The very breeze that sighed through the rushes was the wistful voice of one unwisely reluctant of earthly joy and pain.

It is almost impossible for us—so long saturated with Semitic thought—to recreate for ourselves the mind of the Greeks and Romans fed upon the strength and beauty of a noble pantheism—whose interpretation of life knit their souls to the wholesome earth, and filled them with zest to live and patience to die—whose gods embodied their own lovely ideals of youth immortal, beauty unfading, serene wisdom, the soil's natural wealth, the vine's purple joy. Their attention was fixed upon the present life—their problem how to live it bravely, wisely, richly. All beyond this were uncertain shadows, about which it was impossible to know, and useless to speculate.

Upon the Etruscan tombs, of all mortuary monuments the most lovely, is to be found a revelation clearer than words of the European attitude toward death—those recumbent figures, all grace and peace, carved by the hands of forgotten genius with so inexplicable a skill that the immemorial stone grows deliquescent before one's eyes as if melting and sinking into the mother earth. In them is no sense of struggle or rebellion. They consent to extinction as gently as autumn's last day fades into the silence and darkness of winter. Their season has been fulfilled. They have lived and loved, and they are proudly willing to sink into the elements from which they rose.

It was not until the Asiatic conquests of Alexander brought the mind of Europe into contact with the religions of the East, that this sane attitude was darkened by a conception as radically opposite as the antipodes. Nor did the Roman civilization suffer a shadow upon its manhood until it in turn brought home with its eastern captives that fierce egotism that feared extinction as an irremediable horror. This mind of the other hemisphere could never reconcile itself to the inevitable blotting out of its own individuality. Impossible as it was to deny the incontrovertible fact of death, it conceived, as an escape from the greatest of evils, the idea of the continuance of its identity either in an endless round of reincarnations, or as an impalpable essence triumphant in heaven or defeated in hell. The shadow of their own terror cast upon their imagination the figures of monstrous deities—thousand-armed, myriad-eyed, maleficent, and unakin to themselves. Gods not to be propitiated by song and dance, or the offering of fruit and flowers, but loving to snuff at altars drenched in blood; placated for the sins of the guilty only by the anguish of the innocent, and so meticulous in their tyranny as to require not only the abandonment of all natural appetites, but pursuing even unwitting lapses from submission with eternal and malignant penalties.

Oriental egotism flung itself with equal persistence against the limitations of time, space, and character. In the East arose the systems of magic which sought philosopher's stones, elixirs of youth; which endeavoured to overcome all obstacles through pure intensity of will, and undertook to constrain even the prodigious gods it had itself created by sheer force of its own asceticism and determination.

Rome had been completely honeycombed and corrupted by Eastern mysticism before the final fatal clash of faiths occurred under Constantine, and the Semitic conception of the immortal importance of the human individual overthrew European nature-worship. So potent was this idea that for more than a thousand years Europe lent itself to scorn and repression of nature, and attempted to deal with life as only a pathway to death and the infinitely more important future beyond. The miserable confusion of the Dark Ages was the result of this struggle of the materialistic spirit of the European race in the bonds of a mysticism foreign to its genius.

The Renaissance was rightly named a new birth. Out of the womb of this long night arose once again the mind of the West in its natural shape. Slowly beauty, knowledge, health, regained their old empire. Life grew in importance, and the futile, millennial-long struggle against death began to seem what it truly was—a mere terrified dream of the darkness.

All this appears a long way around to Stevenson, but it is by this avenue I travelled—amid all those soft declamations—to find him the typical poet of the nineteenth century. Stevenson is pure Roman, not a touch of the Semitic is upon him. Every line of his prose and verse attests it. Someone said the other day that Hardy was not so much a pagan as a "revolted Christian," and brought as a charge against him that he did not resent the hard fates of the characters in his books. The second charge, of course, contradicts the first. It was the Eastern rebellion against Fate—against things as they are—that nourished its mysticism. But however one may decide as to Hardy there is no uncertainty as to Stevenson. His relish for life—life with all its pains and limitations—was keen to ecstasy. He leaves no dubiety on that head. Here was no wish for a city of gold and pearl, fenced from care, in which to take the refuge of ease in an impossible Elysium. His "House Beautiful" was

"A naked house, a naked moor"

and

——"the incomparable pomp of Eve"

was all he asked to make desirable "this earth, our hermitage."

That this life leads to nothing more does not daunt him.

> "On every hand the roads begin,
> And people walk with zeal therein,
> But wheresoe'er the highways tend
> Be sure there's nothing at the end."

To which he adds cheerfully:

> "Hail and farewell! I must arise,
>   Leave here the fatted cattle,
> And paint on foreign lands and skies
>   My Odyssey of battle.
>
> "The untented Cosmos my abode,
>   I pass, a wilful stranger;
> My mistress still the open road
>   And the bright eyes of danger.
>
> "Come ill or well, the Cross, theCrown,
>   The rainbow, or the thunder,
> I fling my soul and body down
>   For God to plow them under."

He will allow no mistake as to the purpose of his existence. He cares not what may lie beyond the portals of an undreaded death, but this bright, present existence is for manful struggle; a struggle not maintained in hope of future, or terror of punishment, but because he loves not only

> "Flowers in the garden, meat in the hall,
> A bin of wine, a spice of wit,
> Ahouse with lawns enclosing it,
> A living river by the door,
> Anightingale in the sycamore"—

but loves also to

> "—— Climb
> Where no undubbed civilian dares,
> In my war-harness, the loud stairs
> Of honour ——"

Nothing so moves his scorn as the lazy maggot who shuts himself into the snug nut of his religion and concern himself only to save his own poor, unimportant little soul. Hear the call of his "Lady of the Snows" to the pallid monks uttering prayers and *memento mori*. And Stevenson speaks as does he who knows. It is easy enough for those sitting cozily at home to talk loudly of war and danger, but this was a man who literally fought with death daily. An extract from one of his private letters, written shortly before the end, says:

"For fourteen years, I have not had a day's real health; I have wakened sick and gone to bed weary; and I have done my work unflinchingly. I have written in bed, and written out of it, written in hemorrhages, written in sickness, written torn by coughing, written when my head swam for weakness; and for so long, it seems to me I have won my wager and recovered my glove. I am better now, have been, rightly speaking, since first I came to the Pacific; and still, few are the days when I am not in some physical distress. And the battle goes on—ill or well, is a trifle; so as it goes. I was made for a contest, and the Powers have so willed that my battlefield should be this dingy, inglorious one of the bed and the physic bottle. At least I have not failed, but I would have preferred a place of trumpetings and the open air over my head."

And after a desperate illness, when he rose gasping from the waters of extinction, his first cry on feeling the earth beneath his feet once more were those brave verses "Not Yet my Soul."

He was not upborne by any of that so amazing sense of superiority to the rest of the universe which has aided vain humanity to minimize its defeats. He knew how small was his place in what Carlyle calls "the centre of immensities, the conflux of eternities." Hear him paint what he calls his "Portrait," and he reiterated that his noblest impulses were akin to "a similar point of honour which sways the elephant, the oyster, and the louse, of whom we know so little."

Finally, in the famous Christmas Sermon he sums up in prose the thoughts that breathe through all the varying cadence of his verse—

"Whether we regard life as a lane leading to a dead wall—a mere bag's end, as the French say—or whether we think of it as a vestibule or gymnasium where we wait our turn and prepare our faculties for some nobler destiny ... whether we look justly for years of health and vigour, or are about to mount into a bath chair as a step towards the hearse,—in each and all of these situations there is but one conclusion possible; that a man should stop his ears to paralyzing terror, and run the race that is set before him with a single mind."

In that Sermon is all the philosophy of Greece, the stern courage of Rome.

DECEMBER 23.
"Philistia, be Thou Glad of Me."

Strange things rise up to us out of the deeps. Because I am a heathen, and Apollo is my god rather than any other, I have never been quite able to comprehend the powerful appeal the Hebrew Messiah makes to the hearts of so many. The solution is to be found in this "De Profundis"—Oscar Wilde's posthumous volume. It is a beautiful book: likely to become a classic of our language by reason of its beautiful, limpid English, its amazing exposition of the course of reasoning by which an outcast of humanity reaches peace and reconciliation with his own soul.

The man's crime, I think, was the result of his reluctance to relinquish youth, with its passions and stimulations of the senses. We all find its relinquishment a tragedy. Some of us refuse to accept the slow, cold enveloping of that cruel serpent of Time, which squeezes out of us our beauty, our vigour, our warmth, and leaves us pallid and eviscerated before devouring us entirely. Wilde, whose whole existence was the pursuit of passion and beauty, violently resenting the fact that with the lapse of years he was no longer able to wake the old thrill of existence by any of the old methods—finding that poetry, art, and the beauty of women all left him more and more jaded and cold, he grasped at vice as a means of heat, and brought himself within the iron clutch of the law. One can guess, even without the aid of his own confessions, at the hysterical rage of this sybaritic dandy caught in the grim trap of the reprobation of Society. Not only the physical discomforts and restraints bore heavily, but more intolerable was the contempt and disgust of the average man—the Philistine—to whom he had always held himself airily and scornfully superior. The old primal laws of the struggle for life lie too deep for even the boldest of us to lightly face universal condemnation. The worst of rebels and cynics is so dependent upon the countenance of his fellows that when good-will is withdrawn a sort of madness of despair falls upon him, and this vain, sensitive poet makes it plain how the passionate protest of the ordinary criminal was in his case intensified to ecstasy. One sees the poor creature, like a rat in a cage, darting hither and thither, and shivering with sick and furious helplessness at the rigidity of the barriers by which the world had shut him away from any further part in the body corporate.

In the last exhaustion of his grief a light dawned for him. There was one who had protested against these laws of reprobation which Society had codified—one who had mercy for the sinner; who had insisted that the suffering and sorrow experienced by those not conforming themselves to the pattern

Society demanded regenerated the victims of sorrow, and they became of more worth than those who condemned them. Here was a means of regaining his own peace with himself. Here was a way out of his imprisonment in the scorn of his fellows.

Mary Magdalen, because of her sumptuous repentance, was of more value than the busy and virtuous Martha. The Prodigal Son was more welcome than the patient home-keeper. The lost sheep was the really important member of the flock. The repentant thief was the heir of Paradise. The sinning woman was bid go in peace. All the offenders against the laws of Society were welcomed: the dull walkers in the beaten path were contumeliously branded as Philistines and Pharisees. At once, by this point of view, the prisoner was freed from his cell. It was possible to stand upright once more and return frown for frown with his judges. All these were redeemed by their "beautiful moment"—? Well, let him too have his beautiful moment and he was really of more worth than those who had condemned him.

Here is the secret of the hold the Hebrew thinker has had upon humanity.

When our race slowly began to stand up on their hind legs and to live a life in common, they found—as the ants and bees had done before them—that the common life was only to be made feasible by adopting some general law of behaviour which would enable individuals to assimilate; and so morals and conscience had their generation. A man might never leave his home if the tribe would not accept it as an evil to steal; might never sleep in peace if murder were not a crime; would not feed his children were there not a rule against adultery which ensured him against assuming duties to cuckoos. How bitter, slow, and toilsome was that upward struggle to subdue for the good of the mass the lusts of the individual all history relates. Always a remnant have protested against these hard exactions of the general good at their expense. Always the tribe has, for its own safety, slain, imprisoned, cast out the rebels. The war is not over yet; will, possibly, never end. Always those who prefer their own ends will strive to find justification for their wilfulness; will seek some ground for answering scorn with scorn—and their vociferousness, their lofty, sentimental phrases confuse the minds of the slow-witted.

Alas! dear Philistine—what contumely you suffer at the hands of the revolted! You have grown apologetic for your virtues, which the idealists cast in your teeth as a reproach. You are so foolish you cannot eat of the fruit of desire and at once make it as though it had never been by one "beautiful moment" of emotion. You are so stupid you cannot content the neighbour who owned the fruit by accusing him of being hard because your repentance does not satisfy him for his loss. You are "stodgy"; you are "narrow." You are bitter and untender because you worship the God of Things as They Are, instead of accepting a theism of Things as They Might Be. Of course you really rule the world, and when your critics become too aggressive your logic of stone walls and iron bars makes a trenchant reply, but you are very inarticulate. No one gives you credit for your patient, dull self-restraint. You almost apologize to the scoffers for your persistent moral drudgery. You talk very little about the temptations you have resisted—so much less dramatic than sins against your fellows histrionically washed away by repentant tears. Your painful drudging up the path of obvious duty dazzles and touches no one.—But I, at least, love and respect you—you poor old self-denying Pharisee!

DECEMBER 24.
"Oh King Live Forever!"

Oh, King!—great King
Afar in that pleasant place—
(Sleeping in Avalon,
Island of Queens—)
What are thy dreams?
Where no sound cometh at all
Save the lapping of waves,
Of the lake's waves lapping the shore;
And the moving of winds
Stirring a rustle and ripple of leaves—
An infinite rustle and ripple of leaves—
And lifting a little, a little thy wide-strewn hair
Fadeless and gold—
What are thy dreams?
There where no bird sings,
Nor is any bruit by thy head
Save only the singing of Queens—
Seven and sad—
Singing of swords and of war,
Singing of Carleon—
Singing a magical lay,
Sweeter than lutes,
A song made of magic by Merlin
Dead in the wood....
What are thy dreams, oh King!—
Arthur—thy dreams?
Tristram is dead, and Gawain.
Galahad gone, and Sir Bors.
Merlin is dead in the wood.
The base peasant tramples the mire
That once was the heart and the lips
Of Mordred the base and the liar.
The wind of the Breton coast,
Stormy and sad,
Has blown for a thousand years
The dust of that Knight—
Launcelot's dust—

Dust of his bones—
To and fro in the roads—
And the dust of his sword
Blows in the eyes of brave men passing that way
And stings them to tears.
Oh, dread King, what are thy dreams?
Guinevere is but a name—
Frail, and lovely, and sad.
All whom thou lovedst are gone.
Beauty availed them not;
Courage, nor pride, nor desire.
The sound of their singing is dumb;
The sword is broken in twain;
Magic to folly is turned;
Even love might not avail.
Only the King liveth still—
Only the King
Liveth and dreams.
Only the heart above self—
Only the heart steadfast and wise
Liveth forever in Avalon,
Hearing a song
Always of swords and of war,
But dreaming of Peace,
Dreaming of Honour, oh King!
Dreaming great dreams.

JANUARY 1.
The Little Room.

I remember that long ago when I used to be made to memorize Campbell's sentimental lines on The Exile, beginning,

"There came to the beach a poor exile of Erin"—

they only called forth my unsympathetic infantile jeers; but last spring I went home. Suddenly, as we passed along the tawny marshes lying like great dun lions by the edge of the misty gulf, I realized that for twenty discontented years I too had been suffering the pangs of the Exile. Memories and emotions, so long disused as to be almost forgotten, boiled up with the impetuosity of geysers. Possessions of my secret life that I think I was never really conscious of at all came to life. I haven't the least idea, for example, why the buoyant feathery boughs of the first Southern cedar I saw made me strongly wish to weep lovely, sentimental tears, but I knew at once why I had invariably felt bored with the conventional admiration of mountains. Why, indeed, *should* scenery only be important when perpendicular? To my mind, to have the landscape getting up on its hind legs and hiding the view is simply tiresome. Here one could see everything—could open one's lungs and breathe what the Creoles used to call *la grande air*, and let one's heart go out to the land.

You blessed mother country! Those people where I have lived so long seem not to care particularly for their birthplaces. Their patriotism is satisfied by an immense political abstraction and a striped flag. I have always suspected that if one took off the heads of such folk and looked down inside one would find inside only wheels and coiled springs, instead of flesh and blood. David Yandell used to say, "I'm for the Yandells against the whole world, but if it's between the Yandells and Dave, then I'm for Dave!" One might be for that political abstraction against the world, but between that abstraction and Louisiana, then I'm for Louisiana.

I began to suspect too that some of my heresies and revolts had really been caused by the bitterness of exile, though from the very beginning I have seen the King without his mantle. When my elders handed out to me the accepted platitudes in answer to my early attempts to realize the world in which I moved, I stared at them "in a wild surmise," the aforesaid conventionalities appearing to me to be so at variance with the facts as I saw them. They appeared to me—these elders—to be imagining a King's cloak to cover the world as it really was; to be neglecting and minimizing the things really worth while; to be inventing ideals and standards not in themselves noble.

158

I struggled long against the mask and domino which muffled words and impeded action, but time and the years have made me more patient. I have grown to see that they may have their uses. The average man shrinks aghast from the naked truth, even when it is beautiful. There is a sort of universal prudery that shrinks from the nude in life as well as in art. Perhaps these universal draperies cover as much that is repulsive as it does of the beautiful.

Verestchagin, the Russian painter who was blown up on the Petropalovsk, had three pictures with him when he was in this country that conveyed to me a much needed lesson. He called them "Christ in the Wilderness," "The Sermon on the Mount," and "The Cursing of Jerusalem."—A haggard boy fleeing to the desert for meditation upon the tragedies of existence, for which he is sure there must be some panacea if one could only think it out; the triumphant youth announcing to humanity the solution of all its difficulties; and the disappointed man crying reproachfully to the heedless multitude preferring its own old way—"how often would I have gathered thy children together as a hen doth gather her brood under her wings, and *ye would not!*"

As time cools our cocksureness, more and more is one willing to let the world go its own gait and retire into one's secret life; and there comes at last one day a revelation of the meaning of it all, and this revelation brings peace and poise. The four walls of character and environment are an unescapable prison. Heroic effort will not open a door or break through its blank solidity. One may look out upon the world from one's little room, but there one must live one's appointed time. In youth one does not understand or accept this: then anything seems possible of expansion or change, but *veillesse savait.*

Once this is accepted—not by word alone, but mentally grasped and realized —the disordered, confusing bits of existence fall at once into an ordered pattern. Life must be lived in the Little Room. Others may not enter; one's self may not escape. Action falls within its space and can, therefore, be calmly ordered and planned. One will not undertake aught that is impossible within its compass, and struggle, discontent, and confusion are therefore at an end. And within this inviolate enclosure one is safe and private. To those regarding it from without its appearance is much like that of all the other cubicles, but inside, if one chooses, it may be richly hung, sumptuously adorned, with the treasures of one's secret life. Odd, outworn weapons of opinion may give a martial touch to the walls here and there; treasures brought up from the deep may speak of the wild winds of young fancy, and taste yet of the salt of long dried tears. Soft imaginings may invite the weary head, fine embroideries wrought from the many-coloured threads of life may lie beneath the foot. The prison is, should one choose it, a palace.

Long ago, of a summer morning, threading with soundless paddle and slow-sliding canoe one of the quiet streams that wound like a blue vein across the sunburned breast of those marshes, I found in the deep grasses, that everywhere grew breast high, an illimitable garden of flowers. Looked at from above there was but the smooth, deep fleece of verdure—but thus intimate, close to the warm skin of these vast salt prairies, thousands of beautiful freakish blossoms revealed themselves—many-tinted, heavy as wax, fragile as cobwebs, perfumed, fantastic, multitudinous....

I stared a little, pondering, and then passed on carelessly about my childish business, unrealizing that I had found a picture and a parable to hang, after many years, upon the walls of my Little Room.

JANUARY 2.
Aftermath.

If it might be, Life's harvest being past,
And past the perfect fruitage of the soul,
I yet might gather up some small sweet dole
From out Time's fingers in the wide fields cast—
If it might be that though from out the vast
Blue spaces all the tides of light did roll,
There yet might linger some pale aureole
To faintly flush my western sky at last—
I would forbear youth's lordly large demands,
Nor swallow tears at sight of loaded wains
Of others who all full and rich did go;
Content that I, no more with empty hands,
Might bear across the level darkening lands
My sweet few sheaves home through the afterglow.

Lightning Source UK Ltd.
Milton Keynes UK
UKHW011845181022
410670UK00004B/238